The Princess
and the
Suffragette

Scholastic Children's Book
An imprint of Scholastic Ltd
Euston House, 24 Eversholt Street, London, NW1 1DB, UK
Registered office: Westfield Road, Southam, Warwickshire, CV47 0RA
SCHOLASTIC and associated logos are trademarks and/or
registered trademarks of Scholastic Inc.

First published in the UK by Scholastic Ltd, 2017

PB ISBN 978 1407 18565 1

A CIP catalogue record for this book
is available from the British Library.

Printed by CPI Group (UK) Ltd, Croydon, CR0 4YY
Papers used by Scholastic Children's Books are made
from wood grown in sustainable forests.

1 3 5 7 9 10 8 6 4 2

www.scholastic.co.uk

The Princess and the Suffragette
Holly Webb
SCHOLASTIC

For Tom, Robin and Will – so proud that you are growing up and getting ready to vote

Chapter One

One afternoon in June, a carriage rolled up to the door of a tall house in a quiet London square. The girl who climbed down the steps was dressed in the height of fashion, her dress heavily trimmed with lace. She was swathed in a rich sable stole and she stroked the fur smugly as she looked up at the house and the discreet brass plate by the front door.

Miss Minchin
Select Seminary for Young Ladies

"I have come to visit Miss Jessie," the girl said to the sour-faced parlour maid who answered the door.

"I'm sure I don't know, miss," the parlour maid began. "I'm not sure what Miss Minchin would say. Shall I take in your card to her?"

"Oh, for heaven's sake, Mary," the girl snapped. "It's me, Miss Lavinia. Just show me into the schoolroom." And she tilted her head sideways so that the maid could see underneath her enormous hat.

The parlour maid peered at her, and her mouth turned down even further. "I didn't recognize you, miss," she said coldly, standing back to allow her in. "I'll show you to the schoolroom. As if you didn't know exactly where it was," she added under her breath. She glanced behind her and smirked a little as she watched Lavinia primping in the mirror on the wall, adjusting her hat to show off her sharply pretty face and the elaborate piles of her hair.

"Miss Lavinia to see you, Miss Jessie." The maid threw open the schoolroom door and stepped back to allow Lavinia to swan graciously inside.

"Lavinia!"

"Lavvie! Oh, you've come to visit!"

"Look at your dress, and, oh, Lavinia, the furs! Did your papa buy them for you?"

The girls swarmed around her, cooing and stroking the rich brown fur and admiring the puffs of ostrich feathers on Lavinia's extravagant hat.

"Do you think she put on her very grandest things, just to show off to all of us?" muttered a younger girl, sitting in the deep window seat that looked on to the street. "She looks ridiculous. That hat – she can't even see out from under it without cricking her neck."

"Ssshhh, Lottie, she'll hear you."

"I don't care if she does," Lottie retorted. "It's not as if she can do anything to us now, Ermengarde. Miss Minchin's has been almost bearable since Lavinia left. Jessie isn't nearly so bad without

Lavinia here to egg her on." Lottie watched the others, who were listening delightedly to Lavinia's boasting, and turned back to the window in disgust, watching the dusty, sunny street in front of the seminary.

Almost bearable... Lottie had been at Miss Minchin's since she was a spoiled baby of four. She had grown up in luxury, surrounded by Miss Minchin's grand furnishings, taught French and literature and dancing by the most expensive teachers. She was a Young Lady, through and through, just like Lavinia and the other girls.

She hated it. No one actually liked Miss Minchin's – unless Lavinia had? Lottie glanced back at the crowd in the middle of the schoolroom and frowned. Lavinia had always been a bully, but a clever one. She seemed to know the most hurtful thing to say, at the very worst moment. As a favourite pupil of Miss Minchin's, she was almost unstoppable – certainly Lottie would never dare to complain about Lavinia's cruelty. She had ruled the schoolroom with her sharp tongue and sharper nails. Yes, perhaps Lavinia *had* enjoyed her time as queen of the seminary. She had learned from Miss Minchin herself, Lottie thought. Her cutting remarks were just the same sort of things Miss Minchin said about wrong sums or daydreaming or bitten nails.

The pupils at Miss Minchin's knew quite well who the favourites were. Not the cleverest girls, but the richest ones. The ones who had families that would recommend the seminary, and send more girls to be shut up and stifled in the tall dark house.

The heat had yellowed the leaves on the trees early and there wasn't a breath of wind to move them, but Lottie still ached to be outside. Not in a slow, tortuous crocodile of polite little girls, but running around the square, chasing after a hoop or a ball, as the children from the other houses in the square did sometimes. She sighed, and Ermengarde sighed too.

"Perhaps Jessie hasn't been so awful to you." Ermengarde stroked her cheek nervously with the fluffy end of her plait. "But she never stops telling me how stupid I am. And Lavinia visiting is only going to make her worse."

Possibly Lavinia heard her name – she certainly looked over at just the wrong moment, when Ermengarde was doing her very best impression of a frightened white rabbit, and Lottie had wrinkled her nose in disgust.

Lavinia, seated on one of the schoolroom chairs with her ankles graciously crossed, smiled at them, at her grandest. Her expression was sweet and pitying – the smile of an adult faced with two silly girls. "Is there something the matter, Lottie?" she asked gently. "You look quite ill. Perhaps you should go and see Miss Amelia and ask to be put to bed."

Lottie smiled back. "I do have a little bit of a headache," she admitted. "I'm afraid your necklace is making it worse. It's just so glittery. Paste jewels are very bright, aren't they?"

Lavinia sucked in a breath. "These are real diamonds," she snapped. "My papa gave them to me, for my presentation at court. They are *not* paste!" She managed to plaster her smile on again. "Of course, a *little girl* like you wouldn't be able to tell the difference." She whisked round, and carried on talking to Jessie about her court presentation dress and its eleven-foot train. She was telling the others about all the compliments she'd received, but there were red patches across the tops of her cheeks, and it was easy to see that she was furious.

"I don't think her court presentation can have been that much of a success, if she has to come back to Miss Minchin's and boast to Jessie and all of us," muttered Ermengarde. "Doesn't she have a huge horde of fashionable new friends now that she's a debutante?"

"Ermie!" Lottie nudged her admiringly. "That was almost catty. Well done. Pity you said it to me instead of Lavinia, though."

Ermengarde shuddered. "I can never think of

anything to say when she's actually in front of me, you know that. It's one of the things I miss most about Sara – she knew how to put Lavinia in her place, every time."

Lottie watched thoughtfully as Lavinia showed off the absurd plumes of her hat. "Except that Sara was always so perfectly ladylike about it. She couldn't bear to be as nasty as Lavinia, because she was trying to behave like a princess, and a real princess wouldn't lower herself to be rude. Well, I don't ever want to be a princess – imagine only ever talking to stuffy, idiotic princes! I'll be as rude and common as anything if it gets a rise out of Lavinia." She giggled. "She did mind about that necklace, didn't she? Do you think it *is* real?"

Ermengarde peered at it, trying not to be too obvious. "I suppose so. Her parents are terribly rich. You were probably too little to remember, but Lavinia's clothes were the nicest at the school, until Sara came. I think that's why Lavinia always detested her. Lavinia loved being the one that everyone admired, and Sara's things were so beautiful, no one looked at Lavinia any more."

"I suppose you're right. But even if those are real diamonds, it's just showing off to wear a grand necklace like that to come and visit your old school. Where does she think she is, Buckingham Palace? And it's far too warm to wear sables in June, it's ridiculous. She's put on her dressiest things, just to make us all feel small." Lottie pouted, and turned away to watch the square again. It almost hurt, to be cooped up in the stuffy atmosphere of the schoolroom. "It's worked too," she whispered miserably to Ermengarde. "I do feel small. I hate it here, Ermie. It makes me mean."

"Only Lavinia and Jessie make you horrible," Ermengarde told her firmly. "You're nice to me. And most people aren't. Ignore Lavinia, Lottie. She always was a beast, and growing up hasn't made her any less of one."

"I wish she wasn't so tall."

"You're getting taller."

"She and Jessie and all the older ones still think of me as Baby Lottie, though," Lottie argued, pressing her nose against the window. "Even you and Sara do sometimes, I can see it in the way you look at me. There are lots of younger ones now – Daisy and Victoria and Meg. I can't help being small, and having curls."

Ermengarde smiled at her. "I should think that Lavinia looked quite like you, when she was little. She has blue eyes and fair curls too."

"Ugh!" Lottie shuddered.

"Oh dear, Lottie. I was just coming to say goodbye, but I see your manners haven't improved. What a very unladylike noise." Lavinia gathered her stole around her shoulders, and stood smirking down at the pair of them in the window seat.

"How would you know what's ladylike?" Lottie snapped. "Just because you've left school, it doesn't mean you know everything suddenly. A real lady wouldn't come here wearing diamonds and gloat over us all." Then she smiled at Lavinia, dimples suddenly showing, and her eyes glittering. "Perhaps you could go next door to Mr Carrisford's house and show your diamonds to Sara. I expect she'd like to see them. She could show you some of hers."

Ermengarde pressed her hand over her mouth but Lottie and Lavinia still heard her sputtering with laughter. Ermengarde couldn't hold it back, Lottie realized. It was irresistible. She was smiling herself, even though she could see the dangerous colour sweeping up Lavinia's neck and the ugly expression in her eyes.

"Don't you dare," Ermengarde squeaked, jumping up and pushing Lavinia's hand away, as the older girl went to box Lottie's ears.

Lavinia flounced off to the door, surrounded by a mob of twittering girls. Lottie put her arms around Ermengarde and leaned against her shoulder. "Whenever I tease you, Ermie," she whispered, "just remind me that you did that."

"I did. . ." Ermengarde murmured shakily. "I

actually did. I need to sit down, Lottie, let go of me a minute, my knees have gone all wobbly." She sank back on to the window seat and Lottie huddled next to her.

"I hate Lavinia," Lottie said bitterly. "I hate it here."

"Ssshhh..." Ermengarde said. "Look. Miss Minchin."

The fish-eyed mistress had appeared in the doorway, drawn by the noise of the excitable gang of girls fussing around Lavinia. Or perhaps it was just her nose for trouble. Miss Minchin always seemed to appear whenever anything interesting was happening – usually to stop it at once. Her black silk dress whispered over the polished boards, and Lottie shrank into the cover of the window seat, behind the curtains. She had lived at Miss Minchin's for years, but oddly, each year she grew more afraid of her, not less. A spoiled four-year-old only cared that she wasn't allowed cake at tea – at the age of ten, Lottie saw the hollow coldness behind Miss Minchin's smiles and sweet words.

Miss Minchin's sister, Miss Amelia, was hovering behind her, looking anxious, which meant nothing. Miss Amelia always seemed to be worried about something.

Miss Minchin stood surveying the schoolroom and the chattering died away to an uncomfortable, nervous silence. Then she smiled, her lips stretching thinly. "Miss Herbert. How very pleasant to see you. You have come back to visit your school friends, I suppose? A generous-spirited thing to do." She moved forward, slow and stately, and held out her hand graciously for Lavinia to shake.

Lavinia burrowed into the thick dark softness of her stole, as if she was drawing strength from the expensive fur. It seemed to remind her that she was not a child and had no need to dread Miss Minchin's cutting tongue any longer. Lottie saw her straighten her shoulders and apply a bright, social smile. She extended her hand rather limply, as though it was a great effort, and drawled, "Yes, indeed. It seems such a very long time I've been away. I *have* missed everyone."

"All of a month," Lottie whispered to Ermengarde.

"And you've been presented at court, I believe?" Miss Minchin said approvingly. "What a great honour, to have the chance to appear before Their Majesties." She looked round the schoolroom at the other girls. "Several of you, also, will be presented in due time, girls. I hope Lavinia has impressed you with the need to pay attention in our etiquette classes."

"Oh, yes," Lavinia agreed hurriedly.

"Did you have a beautiful dress, Lavinia dear?" Miss Amelia asked, clasping her hands together and gazing at Lavinia eagerly. Lottie saw Miss Minchin lift her eyebrows slightly. She did not tell Miss Amelia off in front of the girls – or not often – but it was obvious that she thought her younger sister was flighty and far too interested in dresses and jewellery and gossip.

"It was ivory silk," Lavinia told her. "Very simple. But the train makes a huge difference and of course I had white feathers in my hair and the veils." She closed her eyes for a second, remembering her moment.

"Goodness," Miss Amelia sighed. "And did the dear queen look beautiful? You're so fortunate, Lavinia, being presented in the coronation year."

"Beautiful," Lavinia agreed, "but rather stern. She was wearing the most enormous pearl and diamond choker – it made her neck look so long and elegant." Lavinia ran her gloved fingers over her own diamonds, before looking irritably sideways at Lottie. But Lottie was sitting neatly in the window seat, her ankles crossed and her hands folded in her lap, a picture of good manners. She had a gift for annoying Miss Minchin and she didn't feel like being lectured, especially not in front of Lavinia.

Miss Minchin sniffed delicately. She disapproved of diamonds. She wore a mourning pin of her dear departed papa's hair and a cameo brooch on special occasions, but jewellery was not really appropriate for the mistress of a seminary, even a seminary such as hers, for the most select young ladies, from the very best families. Certainly nothing so vulgar and flashy and, frankly, dishonest as diamonds. She was quite disappointed to see dear Lavinia wearing them. For the queen, of course, it was a different matter somehow. . .

"I must go, I'm afraid, Miss Minchin. Papa's carriage was returning to fetch me, I expect it will be outside in the square now."

"Of course," Miss Minchin said, ushering Lavinia out. "Do visit again, Lavinia. So very fortunate for the girls to see one of their classmates fulfilling all the aims of young womanhood."

Lottie turned to look out of the window at Lavinia's carriage. It was there already, drawn up outside the house, the two gleaming chestnut horses stamping up and down.

The window was open at the bottom, just a little – Miss Minchin being a strong believer in the health-giving benefits of fresh air, providing there wasn't too much of it – Lottie pushed it up a smidge further, struggling with the heavy frame, and felt Ermengarde helping her on the other side. "I just want to see the horses," Lottie whispered. Now she could lean her arms on the sill and see out properly. The warmth and brightness of the light in the square half-dazzled her. The sun hardly seemed to make it through the dusty glass into the schoolroom. It was making the brass on the horses' harness glitter.

Lavinia stepped out of the front door, nodding to Mary who had shown her out, and pattered down the steps to the carriage. A servant in a dark coat hurried to open the door for her and the carriage clattered away.

Lottie watched it go with a sigh. However much

she hated Lavinia, at least it was interesting to see her – and her horses were beautiful. Life at Miss Minchin's was the same dull lessons and the same dull squabbles, over and over. The dullness was only brightened by the dancing class and visits to Sara at Mr Carrisford's house next door. Miss Minchin hated Sara and her guardian, but now that Sara was so amazingly rich and the diamond mines she had inherited from her father were so fabulously full of diamonds, she couldn't stop Lottie and Ermengarde visiting. It would be far too hard to explain to their families why they shouldn't go to tea with one of the richest girls in London. Even if Miss Minchin had once turned that same girl into a servant and forced her to sleep in a rat-infested attic. It made visiting Sara even more wonderful, knowing that the mention of the Little Princess Sara must make Miss Minchin feel horribly, deservedly sick.

Tomorrow, Lottie thought, squeezing her hands together excitedly. She was to go to tea with Sara tomorrow.

A flicker of movement below caught her eye and Lottie realized that she had not been the only one watching Lavinia go. Beside the grand stone steps that led up to the front door of the seminary, there was a smaller, dingier entrance for the servants and errand-boys, through the iron gate and down the stairs to the kitchens and scullery in the basement. A small figure was standing on the steps, leaning on the area railings. She wore a rather faded black dress and a grubby coarse linen apron, with a white cap over her straggly greyish-fair hair. One of the maids, Lottie supposed. They changed quite regularly – Miss Minchin was tight-fisted, and did not pay well, and the cook was a horror, bad-tempered and mean. But Lottie had never seen a maid quite so small as this one. Even Becky, the scullery maid Sara had taken with her when she left Miss Minchin's, had surely been older than this girl.

She might even be smaller than me, Lottie thought to herself, which was unusual. Some of the seven-year-olds were as big as Lottie. But surely the new maid couldn't be her own age? Wasn't ten too young to be working?

As if she could feel Lottie staring, the girl turned and looked up at the window. Lottie ducked back hurriedly and let out a mewing cry of pain as she banged her head on the heavy window frame.

"Oh, Lottie!" Ermengarde hugged her and rubbed her hand over Lottie's fair curls. "Whatever did you do that for? You can't have just forgotten about the window?"

"I didn't want her to see me," Lottie gulped, feeling for a lump on the back of her head. "Oh, ow . . . it was embarrassing, I was looking at her, and then she turned round and I just wanted her not to see I'd been staring."

"Well, why shouldn't you look at her?" Ermengarde said, blinking. "She wouldn't complain, Lottie, she's a just a scullery maid. What would she say?"

"Is she a scullery maid, then? Oh, I suppose you can tell from her apron. . ."

"And I know she is, because Becky spoke to her. It was Sara who got the last maid her new situation, you know. Becky told this one – her name is Sally – that if Miss Minchin or the cook mistreated her, she and Sara would help."

"I wonder if Miss Minchin knows." Lottie shuddered. "I'd hate to be Sara if Miss Minchin found out that Sara had been interfering with her servants."

Ermengarde snorted. "Sara was never afraid of Miss Minchin, Lottie, you know that. She would just stare at her when she was being told off, as if she was a princess, and Miss Minchin was, oh, a horrible old prime minister or something like that. You know I'm not good at telling things the way Sara does. Besides, now that Sara is an heiress again, Miss Minchin wouldn't dare say a word against her. She can't risk Sara or Mr Carrisford telling anyone that she turned Sara into a slave while she was poor, can she?"

"I wonder how long this scullery maid will stay

for. I'd simply hate to work for Cook – you can hear her shouting even from up here sometimes."

"She told Becky that it was better than where she was before. She came from some sort of orphanage. She said that little attic room Sara used to sleep in is luxury. She's used to sleeping in a dormitory full of girls and having to work in the laundry. Anyway, someone from the orphanage will come to check that she's happy. If Cook's too horrible, the orphanage people will take her away again and send her somewhere else. They won't be able to get away with not feeding her, like they did to poor Sara."

Lottie shivered. "But she never said, Ermie. I could have given her my dinner, I would have done! All I ever did was give her crumbs out of my pocket for the sparrows round her attic window."

"Sara was far too proud to tell us that she was hungry." Ermengarde sighed. "I didn't notice. I'm not good at noticing, I just let things happen to me. Then as soon as I tried to help, Lavinia told Miss Minchin."

Lottie flushed. "Only because I told Lavinia, but really and truly, I didn't mean to. She was saying horrible things about you, and about Sara. She said to Miranda that it was a good thing you never spoke to Sara any more, she was sure you were much improved. And then I said that was all she knew, you talked to Sara almost every night. . ." She laid a hand on Ermengarde's arm. "You do know that I never meant for her to tell Miss Minchin, don't you?"

"Of course I do, goose." Ermengarde stood up. "I have to go and learn my French vocabulary, Lottie, or Monsieur Dufarge will smirk at me again."

Lottie nodded, and rested her head against the window, gazing across the square, only half-seeing the houses and the occasional carriage rolling by. She was seeing Lavinia instead – that sharp face, sharp nose, lips drawn back from sharp little teeth as she went to slap her. Lavinia looked like a woodland beast, swathed in all those furs. Lottie smiled, imagining the Lavinia-beast slinking away between great dark trees. And then she wrapped her arms around her middle, smiling even more as she remembered Ermengarde protecting her, the way she'd gone pink with amazement and pleasure when she realized what she'd done.

But Lavinia's boasting about her presentation had left Lottie feeling strange and unsettled. However horrible Lavinia was, it was quite obvious that she was the spoiled darling of her family. The diamonds and furs seemed to make that clear, and all the fuss over her appearance at court. Lavinia said her mother had cried at the sight of her in her presentation dress and feathers, and that her older brother had taken charge of her bouquet, fetching the flowers himself from the very best florist in London. It was a side of Lavinia that Lottie had never seen – someone whose family adored her.

Most of the girls at Miss Minchin's were there because their families were out of the country, either living in India, as Sara's father had been when he'd left her at the school, or perhaps stationed abroad with the army. Visits from parents were few and far between, and once girls finished at the school, they often went to join their families abroad and didn't come back to visit. Not that many of them would want to come back and gloat anyway, Lottie thought, wrinkling her nose. That was just Lavinia being Lavinia.

So, most of the time, Lottie didn't feel any different. Ermengarde had relations in England, but Lottie didn't envy her them at all. A series of stuffy, critical aunts visited Ermie on a rota to complain at her and tell her that she was clearly too fond of cake and that her French accent was abominable and her knowledge of English literature needed to be improved at once, it was a disgrace to the family that she was so foolish.

Who would wish for relatives like that? Lottie was certain that it was her aunts, and the disappointed letters from her father (who hardly ever bothered visiting himself) that made Ermengarde so shy and tongue-tied. They told

Ermie that she was stupid, over and over, so Ermie was convinced that they were right. Nicer families would have accepted that schoolwork wasn't what she was good at and praised Ermie for her sweet temper and her friendliness, instead of making her miserable.

It was quite hard not to tease her sometimes, though, Lottie thought, giggling to herself. Ermengarde would believe anything, if one said it with a straight enough face, which was particularly funny in history lessons. When they were studying Joan of Arc, Lottie had convinced Ermengarde that the Arc was the same sort as Noah's, and that the saint had been trying to get the French to build an ark to escape from the English. Miss Minchin had not approved of Ermengarde's account of the battle at Reims.

At least Ermengarde's nasty aunts came to see her, though, and her grumpy, critical uncle. Ermie even went back home to stay with her father every so often. Lottie hadn't seen her father for two whole years. She hadn't been home since she was four years old, when he had left her at Miss Minchin's.

Would she be here until she was seventeen, as Lavinia had been? Another seven years of Miss Minchin's icy sniffs and Miss Amelia's fussing? Lottie drew up her knees, wrapping her arms around them and huddling into the corner of the window seat. Seven years! And then what would happen? Would her father arrange for her to be presented at court, like Lavinia? Would she go back home to live with him? She could hardly remember what the house looked like. How could she call it her home?

Lottie leaned forward, pressing her eyes against the muslin of her dress to hide that she was crying. Suddenly, it all seemed desperately dreary.

Chapter Two

"Lottie, you're here!" Sara came hurrying down the stairs to hug her, swinging her round delightedly. "Oh, it seems ages since you last visited, I missed you." She led Lottie towards the pretty drawing room at the back of the house. "How is Miss Minchin's? Oh, Lottie, whatever's the matter?"

Lottie frowned. "Nothing. Why?"

Sara was gazing at her, with green eyes troubled. "I . . . don't know. For a moment, you looked so sad. Desolate, almost."

Lottie paused, just for a second, before she

smiled and shook her head. She wasn't quite ready to talk to Sara about yesterday. She didn't want to talk to anyone.

Sara turned swiftly at a scrabbling noise from further along the hall. "Boris! Were you begging in the kitchens?" she murmured lovingly, as an enormous dog appeared in the doorway. "You bad dog. Yes, you are." She rubbed her hands over the great boarhound's ears and he gazed up at her adoringly.

"Hello, Boris," Lottie said, a little shyly. She wasn't much used to dogs and Boris was so big, he daunted her. He was the size of a small pony and his jaws were massive. But Lottie had never seen him be anything other than gentle, and he clearly adored Sara. Mr Carrisford had bought him for her and had a silver collar made for him that said, *I serve the Princess Sara*. Boris did look as though he thought he was a princess's dog – he was always so serious.

Boris snuffled politely at Lottie's outstretched

fingers and allowed her to scratch him under the chin.

"You must come and see what Uncle Tom has given me," Sara said, laughing and seizing Lottie by the hand to pull her into the library. "It is the funniest thing."

Lottie followed her eagerly. Mr Carrisford was always giving Sara presents. He had spent two years searching for her after her father had died, desperate to tell his old friend's little daughter that the diamond mine they had owned together was full of diamonds after all, and now half of it belonged to her. He had made himself terribly ill, fretting about the child left alone, and now that he had found Sara, he would do anything to make her happy. The presents he gave her were always beautiful. "Is it another monkey?" Lottie asked hopefully. "You did say that he thought perhaps the monkey needed a friend."

Sara looked back at her, smiling. "No, I told Uncle Tom that I thought one monkey was quite enough. He's so naughty. He slipped out of the front door yesterday and Ram Dass and I had to run around the square chasing him while he leaped about in the trees and threw leaves at us. But Monkey loves this new present too, even though really it belongs to Boris. Boris! Boris! Come on, we'll show Lottie your present."

A new collar, Lottie wondered. Or perhaps a coat, although it was surely too warm for Boris to wear one? But what Sara showed her was a strange, glittering toy building, somehow balanced on the arm of the library sofa.

"We won't disturb Mr Carrisford?" Lottie murmured, looking around.

"No, no, Uncle Tom has gone out to his club," Sara explained. "And if he were here, Lottie, he would be delighted to show you. You know how much he likes people to enjoy his presents."

Lottie smiled. Every so often Mr Carrisford would send her back to Miss Minchin's with a positive armful of bonbons to share with the other girls, or some silly little clockwork toy. Once it had been a whole orchestra of tin instruments and Miss Minchin had made Lottie take them back after Miss Amelia developed a migraine. "I know," she agreed. "But I can't see what it is, Sara. It looks like some sort of small building – like those beautiful Indian shrines you showed me the other week."

"You are very nearly right. You really need to see it in place to understand what it is." Sara nodded mysteriously. "Boris, darling, come here."

The great dog nudged up next to her, his tail waving in excitement, so that it thumped heavily against both girls' dresses. Sara lifted the gilded box from the sofa, and placed it on the dog's back, crouching down to buckle a strap underneath.

"Oh! It's like the things the elephants wear!" Lottie exclaimed. She had seen lots of books about India with wonderful pictures – Mr Carrisford even had a photograph on his desk of him on the back of an elephant, sitting in a little canopied seat.

"I didn't recognize it, until it was on Boris's back. What is it called? I've forgotten."

"A howdah." Sara straightened up, gently pushing the howdah to make sure it was secure. Boris looked around at his back uncertainly, but he didn't seem to mind, even though the howdah must have been heavy.

"Where did it come from?" Lottie asked, admiring the gold paint and the little fringed canopy over the top. The dome of the canopy made the howdah look like a tiny temple on Boris's back.

"Uncle Tom sent for it from India for me. He wrote to one of his friends months ago, asking him to have it made and sending Boris's measurements for the straps. It was a surprise, but he says that he almost told me about it so many times. He couldn't bear waiting. You haven't seen it properly, though, Lottie. Wait a moment, I must find Ram Dass." Sara hurried out, and Lottie heard her calling in Hindustani to Mr Carrisford's Indian servant. There were hurried footsteps, and then a flurry of squeaky chattering noises and Lottie smiled delightedly. Mr Carrisford's little monkey fascinated all the girls at the seminary. Once, when Sara was still working as a servant, he had escaped across the roofs and come in at her skylight window. It had been the monkey who found her, after all Mr Carrisford's searching. Sara had gone next door to take him home and Mr Carrisford had discovered that the child he had been looking for had been in the very next house all along. Whenever the girls at the seminary went out walking or to church, everyone peered at the windows of the house next door, hoping to see the monkey climbing the curtains or simply watching the passers-by.

Now Sara came in with the affectionate creature sitting on her shoulder, clinging to her hair with his wrinkled grey old man's hands. He was chattering away to her as though he knew exactly what he meant, even if no one else did, and as soon as he saw Boris wearing the howdah, he squealed with glee, and sprang on to the great dog's back. He climbed into the padded howdah and lolled there, like some noble traveller.

Boris turned round to look at him, and then looked patiently back at Sara.

"Doesn't Boris mind?" Lottie asked.

"Not if it's only for a few moments." Sara patted the dog's nose gently. "The very first day it came, we did keep it on him for rather too long and he grew tired of it. But he was very good, he simply sat down and let poor Monkey slide out of his seat. Just watch."

The monkey was settled now, and he reached one skinny arm out of the golden howdah and slapped at the gorgeously embroidered cloth, thickly stitched and dotted with tiny mirrors, that protected Boris's back from the tight straps.

Lottie was almost sure that the boarhound sighed. He set off, lumbering slowly around the sofa, with the monkey gazing regally from his gilded throne.

"Miss Sara?"

The two girls looked round and Lottie smiled at Becky, standing by the door in her neat uniform. Becky would never be tall, not after years of half-starving as she grew, but she looked so different now from the yellowish, scrawny thing she had been at Miss Minchin's.

"The tea's served, miss, in the blue drawing room."

Lottie bit her lip. There was a blue drawing room at her father's house. She couldn't call it home.

"Lottie, there's that look again." Sara lifted the howdah from Boris's back and laid it on the sofa. She caught Lottie's arm. "What is it? Don't say that it's nothing. Come on. Come upstairs and have tea with me." She patted Lottie's cheek. "There'll be muffins, Lottie, you know you love them. Then you can tell me whatever is the matter."

Lottie sighed, pulling her face away. Sara would make her tell. She was gentle, always, but so, so persistent. She would strip off Lottie's comfortable layers until she knew the truth. It would be simpler just to tell her.

Sitting in a cushioned chair, with a cup of tea and a plate of muffins at her side, Lottie made one last attempt at distracting Sara. "Ermengarde said that you spoke to the new scullery maid, Becky," she said, as Becky poured Sara's tea.

"Yes, miss." Becky nodded. "Miss Sara thought it might come easier from me, miss. It was a friendly message, like. To tell Sally that she could always come and speak to me if Cook weren't treating her well."

"She has come from the Girls' Village at Barkingside," Sara put in. "They will watch over her, she says. Though I can't say I think much of them, if they sent her to Miss Minchin. Becky, sit down. Drink a cup of tea."

Becky looked towards the door, as though she expected someone to come and catch her out, joining in with the young ladies, but she perched nervously on the very edge of a straight-backed chair, smoothing her apron over her knees. There was a cup set on the tea tray for her, Lottie realized. Sara and her maid must often drink their tea together. Lottie glanced sideways at Sara under her lashes, confused. The older girl had always been a little strange about this sort of thing. She had hated the way that the cook and the other servants bullied Becky, even before she too was reduced to a servant's position at Miss Minchin's. She and Becky had slept next to each other in the cold, dismal attics of the seminary, signalling through the walls to keep their spirits up. After that – of course she couldn't treat Becky as only a maid. But still... Lottie fought down a chilly disapproval that even she recognized was straight from Miss Minchin.

"Becky, how old is she? The new maid?" she asked politely, trying not to sound anything like Miss Minchin.

"Twelve, miss."

"Twelve! But she's so little – she looks smaller than me, I'm sure."

Becky nodded. "She went to the Girls' Village when she was half-grown, miss. They're well-looked after there, but she'd missed a lot of her growing. From not being fed right."

Lottie nodded and pulled her hand into her lap again. She had been about to take another muffin.

"Why did you look so very miserable before?" Sara asked, laying one slim hand on hers.

Lottie blinked, closing her eyes a moment to hold back a sudden and unexpected sting of tears. "Lavinia visited," she admitted slowly, wondering how to explain. "Yesterday afternoon."

Becky made a noise, a sort of disgusted click of her tongue, then she flushed scarlet and apologized. "I'm sorry for interrupting, miss."

Lottie nodded. "I feel like that too. Oh . . . it's silly. It wasn't that she did anything awful – though she did try to box my ears, and you'll never guess, Sara, Ermie slapped her hand away."

"Ermengarde did?" Sara looked shocked and

delighted at the same time, her grey-green eyes sparkling. "Oh, Lottie, how brave of her!"

"Yes, she was so surprised at herself that I think she was almost sick afterwards. But that wasn't it, Sara. Lavinia has been presented at court." Lottie put her head on one side, distracted by a sudden thought. "Will you be, do you think, when you're old enough?"

Sara shrugged. "I expect so. Mr Carmichael – Uncle Tom's lawyer, you know – I'm sure his wife would present me." She wrinkled her nose. "It takes hours, sitting outside the palace in a carriage waiting. All that fuss. . ."

"Yes . . . but Lavinia made such a thing of it, Sara. Her family were so delighted for her. And I thought – " she swallowed – "what will I be like when I'm seventeen or eighteen? What will I *do*? I haven't been back to my father's house in so long, though I suppose that's where I'll go. I don't belong there, Sara! I don't want to spend another seven years at Miss Minchin's, but there might be even worse. Now that I've thought of it, I can't stop thinking of it, and every so often, it simply sweeps over me."

Sara nodded. "Yes," she said quietly. "It does. I remember."

Lottie laughed, a little apologetic crow. "I know it's nothing compared to what happened to you – and the way they treated you too, Becky. But sometimes I feel as if I don't have a home either. No one . . . *wants* me."

"But your father. . ." Sara faltered. "You have a father, Lottie."

Lottie forced out a whisper. "He pays Miss Minchin a great deal to keep me here. I've never been home, not since he first brought me to the seminary when I was four."

"Four!" Becky exclaimed. Then she flushed scarlet, leaning back as if she expected to be shouted at.

"I know." Lottie sniffed. "Six years."

"But why. . ." Sara stopped, uncertainly. "I

remember, when I first came to Miss Minchin's, it was only a little after you. You told me you hadn't any mamma. You used to say it often. I suppose that's why he sent you there, after your mamma died. He thought the seminary would give you somewhere more homelike, with other girls."

"And Miss Minchin as a mother?" Lottie giggled, half-laugh, half-sob. "He wanted to get rid of me. He didn't know what to do with me."

"Perhaps – perhaps he was grieving."

Lottie sighed and nodded. "Maybe. I don't know. I've never talked to him about it – about her. I used to beg him in my letters to tell me about her, because I was forgetting what she looked like, even. But he won't. He never mentions her."

Sara frowned, a deep crease appearing between her eyebrows. "My papa used to tell me about my mamma often," she murmured. "He spoke to me in French, because she was French, and he would tell me stories about her. Even though I never met her, she still seemed to me like a friend, just one who had gone away and might come back one day soon."

Lottie smiled. "Do you remember telling me about her? That she and my own mamma were in heaven, gathering up lilies? Oh, and then Lavinia said that you were wicked, for making up stories about heaven." She brushed the tears off her cheeks. "You told her she'd never know if they were true because she'd never get there."

Becky snorted with laughter, and then pressed her hand over her mouth. Sara flushed pink. "Oh, I didn't . . . did I? Lavinia always tried to be so superior. She did make me lose my temper sometimes, I suppose."

"Yesterday I told her she ought to go and compare her diamonds with yours. That's why she tried to box my ears. It would have been worth it, though, even if Ermie hadn't stopped her."

Sara shook her head, but Lottie could see that she was laughing.

"I dream about my mother, you know," Lottie

said suddenly. "About that story you told, that she's in heaven. I see her walking through the fields of lilies. They're tall and white and so is she. She's walking towards me with a great armful of lilies and she sees me and she drops them and the golden dust of the lilies is all over her white dress, but it doesn't matter. Nothing matters, she's laughing and laughing because she's so happy to see me."

"Oh. . ." Sara whispered.

"Everything's white and gold and green – and when I wake up, for a moment I can still hear her laughing. It's so real, Sara."

"Do you remember her at all, miss?" Becky put in.

Lottie blinked at her.

"For real, I mean. Before she was taken. I never lived with my ma, I had an aunt brought me up. But I do remember one or two things. That's a comfort."

"I – yes." Lottie nodded. "Only a little. I

remember her holding me. I do remember her laugh – I think. But I don't know! What if it's only the dream that I remember? I don't even have a photograph."

Sara stood up and crossed quickly to Lottie's chair, sitting down on the arm and leaning over to hold her. "Do you remember what else I said, when I told you about our mothers and the lilies?"

Lottie sighed and leaned against her. "That you'd be my mamma and your doll Emily would be my sister. But that was only because I was a horrible little brat of a four-year-old having a tantrum about brushing her hair."

"You were very cross." Lottie could hear that Sara was smiling – her voice changed. "Miss Amelia was quite desperate. But, Lottie, I loved fussing over you. Pretending that you were my little girl meant that I had someone to love when I was missing Papa so badly. And when everything changed, you stayed, you and Becky and Ermengarde. Even though you were only seven, you climbed all the way up the stairs to the attics and found me."

"The sparrows," Lottie snuffled.

"Yes, we fed the sparrows." Sara hugged her tighter. "Perhaps sisters instead, Lottie, now that you're too old to want a pretend mamma? Then whatever happens with your papa, you will have someone. All of us are motherless, you and Becky and Ermengarde and I. We should be sisters."

Lottie sighed and rubbed her cheek against the smooth green silk of Sara's sleeve. "Yes," she whispered.

Dearest Papa,

I went to visit Sara at Mr Carrisford's house today. He had given her a pretty howdah for her dog Boris, like an elephant wears, and we played with Boris and Mr Carrisford's monkey.

Papa, would you come to visit me soon? It will be my birthday next month, in July, I shall be eleven. I would so love to see you. Perhaps I could even come home to visit you? I have been counting up and I realize that you haven't seen me for two years, not since my ninth birthday.

I want so much to talk to you about Mamma and what she was like. I know it seems odd to say I miss her now, when she's been gone such a long time, but I do find myself thinking about her more and more. Do you have a photograph of her that I could keep here at school? Sara and I were talking about our families and I find I can hardly remember what Mamma looked like.

A tear splashed on to the letter, blotching the writing she had tried so hard to keep neat, and Lottie laid down her pen with a frustrated sigh. This was the third draft already, and it wasn't any better than the previous two, even without the blotches. She had been trying to write this letter ever since she had returned from Sara's house, and she was beginning to think it would never be done. What she really wanted to write was, *Why do you never mention her? Why do you keep me shut away here out of sight? Are you ashamed of me? Don't you love me?*

But if she sent a letter like that to her father, he would be furious. He would probably write at once to Miss Minchin, demanding an explanation. Miserably, Lottie crumpled the sheet of writing paper and aimed it at the fireplace. The fire wasn't lit yet, but one of the maids would come soon, she expected. Yesterday's sunshine had disappeared and there was a chill rain falling. Her bedroom felt cold already.

Slumping back in her chair, Lottie wondered if she should bother to start the letter again. She would have to write to Papa on Sunday afternoon, anyway; that was when everyone wrote letters home, with Miss Minchin patrolling between the rows of desks so that she could read over their shoulders.

There was a clattering at the door, and the same small scullery maid she had noticed the day before came in with a coal box. She muttered something about, "Make up the fire, miss," and Lottie nodded. She didn't look at the girl – she still wasn't sure whether the maid had seen her watching from the window. Perhaps she had laughed at Lottie bumping her head on the frame. Instead Lottie snatched up another sheet of notepaper, jabbed her pen into the inkwell and tried to start the letter again.

My dear Papa,

Would you consider coming to visit me soon? It will be my birthday shortly and I will be eleven. I would very much like to see you.

She stopped, resting her chin on her hand and staring vaguely across the room, until a faint rustling sharpened her gaze.

The maid was kneeling by the fireplace, reading her letter!

"How dare you?" Lottie meant to shout, but it came out as a squeak.

The girl hurriedly shoved the letter on to the sullenly glowing fire, and stared at Lottie, her face a smooth blank.

"You were reading it! You were! That's a private letter!"

"I just picked it up, miss. There was papers all over. I just picked them up and put them in the fire." She gazed back at Lottie, widening her eyes a little, as though she didn't understand.

Lottie shook her head furiously. "Don't lie! It was all crumpled up. I crumpled it and you flattened it out. I saw – you were reading it."

"I never." But the girl – Sally, Lottie remembered her name was now – was starting to look shifty. She swept the hearth quickly and banged her dustpan and brush back on top of the coal box. Then she stood, making a fuss of wiping her hands on her apron so she didn't have to meet Lottie's eye.

"You're not going," Lottie snapped, jumping up from her writing table and darting across the room to the door. "Not till you tell me what – ow!"

"Oh lord, miss!" Sally was staring at her in horror now. "What did you do? I never touched you, honest I didn't."

"It wasn't you," Lottie snarled, made furious by the pain. "It was me. I tripped over that stupid rug." She scrambled up, rubbing her bruised knee and hissing to herself, and limped over to the door. "Why were you reading it? Oh, I'm not going to complain to Miss Minchin, I just want to know. Do you think she'd listen to me anyway?"

"I picked it up to help light the fire, that's all. I didn't mean to read it. It caught my eye, about the elephants. I saw a picture of one of them, in a book. I thought for a minute you meant they had an elephant next door, miss, I swear that's all it was."

"How could they have an elephant?" Lottie rolled her eyes and snorted. "In a house?"

"Well, they've got a monkey, 'ent they? And that great monster of a dog. I didn't know." Sally glared at her sulkily.

"Did you read the rest of the letter?" Lottie

demanded, and Sally shifted her feet. "Most of it," she admitted. "I just sort of kept on."

"Oh. . ." Lottie blushed scarlet and pressed her hands to her cheeks. "How could you?" The thought of this girl feeling sorry for her, reading her pleading letter. It was horrible. "You're not to pity me," she snapped.

"Pity you?" The maid stared back at her, her mouth hanging a little open. "What would I pity *you* for, miss?"

"For . . . for not having seen my father," Lottie faltered. "That I've been here for so long, without going home."

Sally pressed her hand against her mouth, and Lottie thought for a moment that she was shocked – horrified, perhaps, by Lottie's awful situation. But then she realized that the girl was laughing. Definitely, this time. She was laughing at her!

"Oh!" Lottie stamped her foot angrily. "Stop it! Stop it, or I will tell, I will!"

Sally's face hardened. "You said you wouldn't. You're all the same. Spoiled little princesses, the lot of you."

"I'm not. . ." Lottie shook her head. "You don't know anything."

"I know you've got a room like this," Sally retorted. "And it's my job to sweep it and make your bed and lay your fire and carry your washing downstairs. Who do you think empties your chamber pot?"

Lottie flinched. Miss Minchin and Miss Amelia were always complaining about her manners, but she would never speak about something like that.

"What would I pity you for?" the maid snarled. "Your father's paying for all this, miss, even if he isn't taking you out to tea like the other precious young ladies."

Lottie looked around the room, at the comfortable bed and the writing table and the glowing fire. Her wardrobe, the door hanging a little open. Her frocks were chosen for her by Miss

Amelia, and paid for in her father's bill. Lottie complained about them – Miss Amelia liked white for young ladies, or pale, pretty colours, and too many frills – but they were good and they fitted her nicely. The bed was plain and a little battered and the rug had an ink stain on it, but Lottie had seen the attic where Sally slept, when it had been Sara's. It was cold and there were rats in and out of the holes in the walls. There was never a fire in the iron grate. Sally's dress was too big for her and one of her boots was losing its sole. Her face was smudged with coal dust, and under the dirt it was pale and thin, with bruise-like smudges of tiredness under the eyes.

Lottie looked down at her soft white hands and muttered huskily, "I didn't think." Even after what Becky and Sara had told her, she had hardly thought of the maid as a girl like herself. Until she'd realized that Sally might be thinking about *her.*

"I got to go, miss. I got other rooms to do."

"Yes. I'm sorry, you should go." Lottie stood away from the door, and then leaned over to open it as Sally picked up the heavy coal box.

"I'm sorry," she murmured again, as the other girl slipped out. But Sally didn't even look back.

Chapter Three

"It looks terribly ... serious," Ermengarde said doubtfully, examining a coloured plate of *Henry VII Crowned on Bosworth Field*. "Like a history lesson."

"Well, it was rather long," Charlotte admitted, glancing at her sister. "But so grand! There were five hundred people singing, weren't there, Bella?"

"And the costumes!" Bella sighed dramatically, and Lottie remembered that she had been one of those most impressed by Lavinia's absurdly feathered hat. "Velvet cloaks and crowns and swords. Even the horses were dressed up. We were there all day, looking at everything, and then we spent the night at a hotel with our grandmamma. It was lovely, even if we did have to keep running in out of the rain showers. Will you go to the Festival, Ermie?"

"If it's improving and educational, I expect my uncle might take me, or Papa," Ermengarde said gloomily. "They'll probably expect me to know about all the history. Could I borrow this, Charlotte? If I read it first" – she stared down at the tiny print unenthusiastically – "I might at least have some idea of what's happening. Enough not to look a complete dunce."

Lottie looked at Charlotte's souvenir booklet. She didn't desperately want to watch a pageant all about the history of London, but the Festival of Empire itself sounded exciting. She would like to see the showground at the Crystal Palace, and the buildings from all over the Empire. There were so many exciting entertainments being put on for the coronation and it seemed that she wasn't going to see any of them. Her papa hadn't sent her a souvenir medal or even a mug painted with George V's face. What was the point of living through what all the newspapers were calling "a momentous event in British history" if you weren't allowed to see any of it? *Perhaps I'll buy my own mug*, she thought to herself. *Even if I do think George V is rather ugly, with that horrid pointed beard.*

"Girls!" Miss Amelia was in the doorway, looking flustered. "Since the weather has cleared, we shall go out for a walk before your dinner. Fetch your hats, please, and umbrellas, in case we should be caught in another shower like yesterday's."

There was a chorus of moans – lessons were finished for the day and most of the girls had been gossiping or reading or writing letters. Walks at the seminary were neat and tidy affairs, with all the girls walking two by two in a crocodile, led by Miss Minchin or Miss Amelia, and with another mistress at the back to chivvy everyone along.

There was no chance to run and bowl a hoop in the park or stroke a passing dog, or even to stop and look at anything interesting in the shop windows. But Lottie jumped up eagerly. At least they would be outside, and the dry, dusty pavements were rain-washed now. There would be the strange musky smell of wet dust, and the poor stunted London trees would be fresher and greener for the storm. Lottie dashed upstairs to her room to fetch her jacket and hat, so keen to get out of doors that she almost knocked over someone coming down.

"Oh! I'm sorry, Sally."

The maid was almost invisible behind a large wicker basket of washing that she had obviously been collecting from the girls' rooms. Lottie retrieved a fallen petticoat and balanced it back on top of the pile. "I didn't see you," Lottie explained apologetically.

Sally peered at her around the washing. "Blind, are you?" she muttered irritably. Then she seemed to catch herself at it and bobbed a curtsey awkwardly with the basket. "Excuse me, miss, for getting in the way."

"You didn't, it was my fault, I wasn't looking. Don't pretend to be all polite when I know you aren't." Lottie caught hold of one handle of the heavy basket, seeing Sally struggle with the weight of it.

"Thank you, miss," Sally muttered. "I need to get this down to the scullery, miss, it's my afternoon off." She pulled away from Lottie as the other girls began to straggle up the stairs to fetch their things.

Lottie watched her go, then hurried on up to her room, wondering what Sally would do on her free afternoon. Would she meet up with friends from her orphanage? There must be other girls out in service, who had been in the same home. But then, there was no saying that they would be anywhere close. Perhaps Sally would just walk in the park or go staring in the windows of the shops. Lottie pulled on her flowered straw hat and frowned to herself. Sally would probably snap at her again if she said it, but she envied the maid. No one was going to make her walk in a neat crocodile, with *no swinging of that umbrella, young lady,* and polite topics of conversation chosen by Miss Minchin. She had the afternoon to herself, to wander wherever she liked.

Not that there was that much of the afternoon left, Lottie realized, since it was past four o'clock already. Probably Sally had been set too many tasks to get done that morning and she wasn't allowed out until she had finished. It was stupid to envy her, Lottie told herself firmly. *Think of that attic. And she envies* me*! Warm and well-fed and nicely dressed, with my perfectly furled umbrella. I'm being silly.* She swung the umbrella defiantly, to the shock of two of the smaller girls walking sedately along the passage, and smiled to herself as she raced back down the stairs.

They assembled neatly in the hallway, two by two, to be examined by Miss Minchin for umbrellas and gloves and general tidiness. The seminary had always to make the right impression – it was unladylike to talk too loudly, to slouch, to rattle one's umbrella along the iron railings of the square. The list went on for ever.

At last, after reprimanding Jessie for her wrinkled stockings, Miss Minchin led the way down the stone steps and on to the street. Lottie, in the middle of the column, peered over Jessie's shoulder, trying to work out where they were going. Walk Number Two, she decided, as Miss Minchin turned right going out of the square. About a mile, along Kensington Road around the outside of Hyde Park – with plenty of time to admire the lawns and the flowerbeds from a distance, without actually being able to enjoy them. Lottie sighed and stomped on.

The park looked temptingly green after the rain and the girls slowed to look, admiring the roses and envying the other children running over the lawns. Lottie was peering through the railings at a fountain when she heard Miss Minchin calling crossly, her voice higher than usual. She sounded almost scared.

"Girls! Girls! Turn around. Amelia, do have a little sense – turn around at once!"

Lottie turned away from the railings, and saw that a crowd was streaming past them. There was a sound of music in the distance.

"Oh! Is it a coronation procession?" she asked Louisa, her partner on the walk. Perhaps she wouldn't miss all the celebrations after all.

"I don't know. Lottie, don't follow Miss Amelia, let's pretend we haven't heard. I want to see. There are so many people. Oh, stand back!" Louisa seized Lottie's arm and hauled her backwards as a pair of young boys came bolting past, nearly knocking her over.

Lottie leaned against the railings, breathless, and realized that the whole crocodile of girls was slowly being separated by the crowd – they didn't need to pretend that they couldn't follow the others, the mass of people really *was* pulling them away from Miss Amelia and Miss Minchin. She spotted Ermengarde, holding on to her hat and looking frightened, and reached out to wave at her. "Ermengarde, Ermie, over here!"

Ermengarde nodded, relieved, and began to elbow her way through the press of people towards them. "What's happening?" she hissed. "There's a man on a horse, in *armour*, did you see?"

"No! Oh, this is dreadful, I can't see anything," Lottie said crossly. "Ermie, push me up here on the wall, look, and then I can pull you up, and you too, Louisa."

"We shouldn't... What will Miss Minchin say?" Louisa asked, suddenly remembering her manners – or the number of times she'd been told off about a lack of them, at least. She eyed the low wall that supported the park railings doubtfully.

"Nothing!" Lottie rolled her eyes. "She isn't here to say anything, is she? I don't know where she's got to, or Miss Amelia. They won't ever know we climbed on a wall. And if someone does tell them, we can just say that we were scared of being knocked down by all these people. We were protecting each other."

"I suppose. . ." Louisa agreed.

Ermengarde shrank against Lottie as the crowd swelled and cheered around them. "I think I *am* scared. Here, Lottie, lean on me and jump."

Lottie hopped on to the wall, and leaned over to haul up Ermengarde and Louisa. The three of them stood with their backs against the railings, looking down on the crowd surging past.

"Do you think they're all trying to find places to see?" Lottie murmured to Ermengarde. "Oh, I can see the man on the horse now." She frowned. "Ermie, that's not a man, it's a *lady*. And so is the person leading the horse, the one who looks like Robin Hood."

Ermengarde peered over, blinking short-sightedly. "Is it? Yes, I suppose it is. How very strange! Look at her legs, Lottie!"

"Why are they dressed up?" Lottie stood on tiptoe, leaning out from the railings to try and see better. "I know! She's Joan of Arc."

"Oh. . ." Ermengarde frowned. "Lottie, are you teasing me again? Is this a trick? You're going to try and confuse me about Noah, aren't you?"

Louisa snorted with laughter, but Lottie shook her head. "No, no, I promise. I really do think she's dressed as Joan of Arc. Why else would they have a girl wearing armour? Who are all those ladies following her?"

"They're Suffragettes," Louisa gasped. "They must be. They were in Miss Minchin's paper. And my mamma said something about them when I last went home. But . . . there are hundreds and hundreds of them. I thought there were only a few – Mamma said that no good woman would ever think of being a Suffragette, they were shameful and unwomanly."

"They look grand." Lottie bounced on the wall. "All these ones have silver flags, look! *From Prison to Citizenship*, that huge banner says. Have they been to *prison*, Louisa?"

"Well, I don't know!" Louisa peered at it. "I suppose so. Miss Minchin was showing us the coronation details in the *Morning Post*, and there was something about a court case. They break windows, you know. Suffragettes are not at all ladylike."

Lottie watched the line of women marching past. They were almost all wearing white dresses with coloured sashes and ribbons, and pretty hats – not quite as big and feathery as the hat Lavinia had been wearing a few days before, but along the same sort of lines. They looked extremely ladylike to her. In fact, they looked very like all the mothers and elder sisters who came to visit the seminary. She glanced at Louisa. "Are you sure?"

Louisa shrugged. "I'm only saying what Mamma said. And they made Father so cross that he told my sister Daisy she had to take back her new hat, because it had purple ribbons on it."

The coloured sashes that the women marching were wearing all seemed to have green and purple stripes down them, Lottie noticed. So Suffragettes had their own colours. She definitely ought to make more of an effort to look at Miss Minchin's newspaper, though it wasn't meant for the girls to read. Miss Minchin occasionally read articles out, if she approved of them, that was all.

"Do you suppose we ought to go back to school?" Ermengarde asked worriedly, after several more contingents had gone past, all carrying banners, beautifully embroidered with pictures and slogans. "I think we've been out for ages."

"We can't," Lottie pointed out. "Look at all these people. We'd never be able to get through." She let go of the railings with one hand and patted Ermengarde's shoulder. "We won't get into trouble, Ermie. We'll just say that we were caught up in the crowd. It's true, anyway."

"I suppose so," Ermengarde murmured. Then her eyes widened. "Lottie, Louisa, look at the hats these ladies are wearing! The same as the Welsh women in those pictures of national costumes that Miss Amelia has. And they have dragons on their signs. They must be from Wales, do you think? Can they really have come all that way?"

"The Welsh flag has a dragon," Lottie agreed. "There's another band coming." Lottie frowned. "I don't know what they're playing." The music was echoing around the street, cutting through the excited chatter and whooping from the crowd. It was eerie, almost wailing, and Lottie had never heard anything like it before.

"Bagpipes," Ermengarde said, shuddering. "I hate them. So dismal."

Louisa tittered. "You mustn't say that to Miss Minchin, Ermie, they were Queen Victoria's favourite. Though it does sound like someone crying to me."

It did – but Lottie could feel the music vibrating over her skin, twisting something inside her. Perhaps it was the uncertainty that had come upon her over the last few days, the sense that the world was not as safe and solid as she had always expected it to be, but there was a tightness in her throat as she watched the girl pipers march by in their tartans. They were followed by a float, pulled by two white horses and draped in yards of white fabric and garlands of flowers. More young women in loose white dresses were arranged around the sides. On the top were two figures, to Lottie's eyes rather delicately balanced, and two young girls sitting at their feet, surrounded by flowers and bushes.

"How do you think you get to be up there?" Lottie murmured to Ermengarde, and her friend blinked back in surprise.

"Well, I suppose they're somebody's daughters," she said doubtfully. "But you wouldn't want to, Lottie, would you?"

"No. . ." Lottie said sadly. Somebody's daughter. She wondered what her papa would think of all this. The girl on the front of the float looked shy, as though she hadn't expected to see people crammed all along the road and waving to her.

"She can see us," Lottie whispered, realizing that the girl was watching them, just as they were watching her. She waved and the girl stared gravely back, her hands folded neatly in her lap. She did smile, just a very little, but that was all.

"Lottie Legh!" Louisa leaned closer to her. "You'd better not tell Miss Minchin you'd like to be part of a Suffragette parade."

"It's just pretty," Lottie tried to explain. "More than that – it's so grand. All these people, marching together. Doesn't it make you feel something inside?"

"Hungry," Louisa sighed. "I wonder if they'll keep dinner for us? It isn't really our fault we'll be so late. The crowd's easing off now, don't you think? We could try to get down and walk back to Miss Minchin's."

Ermengarde nodded, and the two older girls climbed cautiously from the wall, holding out their hands to Lottie.

"I suppose we should. . ." Lottie peered one last time over at the parade, wishing they could stay until the very end. The long white column seemed to stretch for ever, banners and flags swaying. Reluctantly, she jumped down to the pavement and caught Ermengarde's hand as they began to thread their way between the knots of people.

"Your dress has marks all over it," Louisa pointed out, as they turned into a quieter side street.

Lottie sighed and held out her white skirts. She only had to look at dirt and it seemed to transfer to her dresses. Miss Amelia would scold – again. "I couldn't help it, the railings were dusty. You and Ermie are almost as grubby as I am." She narrowed her eyes. "We'll just have to say that we were pushed and jostled so much we brushed our dresses against a wall." She hurried ahead, not wanting Louisa's grumping to spoil the memory of the women in their white dresses, the proud, determined faces, and that eerie music.

Another girl was walking along the road in front of them, and for a moment Lottie wondered if it was someone else from Miss Minchin's caught in the crowd as they had been. Then she saw that the girl had long skirts, even though she was only the same size as Lottie, and the fabric was faded, and darned in places. She turned her face away as Lottie came up beside her, but Lottie knew who it was.

"Were you watching the parade too?" she asked Sally.

The maid gaped at her and fumbled anxiously at her jacket. Lottie frowned, trying to see what she was doing and why she seemed so worried. Did she think Miss Minchin wouldn't approve of her servants going to see a Suffragette parade? "We got caught up in the crowd too," she tried to explain. "I don't think anyone will be cross – you couldn't help it."

"What?" Sally had finally managed to take off whatever it was she'd been wearing on her jacket. She stuffed it quickly into the pocket, but not before Lottie caught a glimpse of green and purple.

Lottie's eyes widened, and she put her hand on Sally's arm. "Is that—"

"Leave me alone!" Sally hissed. "It's nothing to do with you!" Then she broke into a stumbling run, leaving Lottie staring after her.

"Who was that?" Louisa asked curiously, as she and Ermengarde caught up with Lottie.

"No one." Lottie shook her head. "I knocked into her by accident. She was annoyed with me. Come on."

The three girls pounded up the stone steps to the seminary and pulled the bell. Miss Amelia answered it herself and shrieked. "There you are! You bad girls, where have you been?"

"It wasn't our fault, Miss Amelia." Louisa immediately began to whine. "There were so many people, we couldn't get through and we didn't know what to do. Lottie got knocked over."

Lottie blinked. Louisa's lying was surprisingly believable – it sounded as though she'd had practice. Lottie tried to make her face look like someone who'd been knocked down and showed her dust-stained skirt to Miss Amelia sadly.

"Oh dear, you poor little thing," Miss Amelia murmured. "Come along in, girls, hurry. We've been so worried about you. My sister was just about to telephone for the police."

"Amelia! Are they here? Why didn't you tell me at once?" Miss Minchin steamed out of her sitting room, white-faced.

"I was coming to tell you, sister," Miss Amelia said sharply. "They were caught up in the crowds and couldn't get back."

"What nonsense," exclaimed Miss Minchin. "They have been running about the streets like hoydens. They must go to bed at once."

"But we haven't had any dinner!" Louisa moaned. "Please, Miss Minchin. . ."

Lottie stayed silent. Miss Minchin didn't like

her, and if she whined too, they'd probably be sent upstairs at once.

"Maria," Miss Amelia said, her voice lowered. "Don't. Let them have their supper."

Miss Minchin's lips thinned so much that they almost disappeared. But she nodded and turned away, her black silk dress swishing as she marched back into her sitting room.

"Thank you, Miss Amelia," Ermengarde whispered, but Miss Amelia glanced nervously towards her sister's door, before waving them away to the dining room.

Chapter Four

Dearest Lottie,

I regret to say that I will not be able to visit you for your birthday. The work of the estate keeps me very busy, and of course I need to be prepared for the grouse shooting. I have written to Miss Minchin, asking her to arrange for a suitable present. She is far more likely to know what is suitable for a young lady of eleven than I am!

Lottie's fingers tightened on the letter, and the thick paper strained and creased. One nail dug in a tiny hole. She had been almost sure that he would come, and her birthday was in two days' time. She had been waiting – for a letter – or even for a summons to Miss Minchin's sitting room to see him.

She had begged. She shouldn't have to beg, should she?

Something fluttered and coiled inside Lottie's chest as she thought, *Would he have sent me away if I were a boy?*

If she were a boy, he would have kept her. He would have known what to do with her, instead of packing her off to Miss Minchin as a motherless and inconvenient four-year-old. Her hands shaking, she forced herself to continue reading the letter.

> *However, I have also sent her a small amount of money, for you to choose a pretty trinket for yourself, with Papa's love. It is a great comfort to me, Lottie, that you are lodged with Miss*

Minchin, a lady of good breeding and high moral standards, when I read in the newspapers of the antics of these disgraceful women, disrupting the capital with their ridiculous parade.

"It wasn't ridiculous," Lottie murmured. "It was beautiful. They were all beautiful. And it was so exciting. How can you say that, when you didn't even see?"

Even though she resented being exiled from her father's house to Miss Minchin's, Lottie had still always assumed that he was right. That his reasons were sound. He couldn't look after a little girl properly, so he had sent her to someone who could. It was much better for her to be surrounded by girls her own age than running wild in a lonely house. Adults were right. Her father was right – it was the way things were.

Except . . . about this one strange little moment, he was clearly wrong. Lottie *had* been there, she *had* seen. And she knew.

This cast doubt on the other things – and Lottie's fragile understanding of the world rocked even further. The rest of the letter seemed to be the same dutiful questions her father usually asked about her schoolwork and her friends. There was nothing important. Lottie laid it down on her writing desk and folded her hands in her lap, her head hanging. She was nothing important either. It had never been so obvious before.

Lottie had not been up the attic stairs for years – and back then, when she had made the decision to keep climbing and climbing until she found her Mamma Sara, she had only made the journey once. But she still knew, vaguely, where the attic stairs were. It was simple just to keep on climbing. At the age of seven, it had seemed a great effort to get all the way up those stairs, and perhaps after a long day of running everyone's errands it still would be. Lottie's breath was coming a little fast by the time she reached the tiny landing outside the two attic rooms.

There was a faint light coming from under one door – from an oil lamp, or perhaps a candle. Lottie glanced back down the stairs, biting her lip. She didn't want to barge in on one of the other servants. But she was almost sure that their rooms were all on the floor below. It was only the scullery maid, the least important servant in the house, who slept in these dismal rooms.

She knocked lightly on the door and then turned the handle, slipping quietly inside. Sally was lying on her bed, still dressed, but obviously half-asleep. She sat up, trying blearily to push her cap straight, and blinked at Lottie.

"What are you doing up here?" she muttered. "Get back downstairs before you're missed. You'll get me in trouble."

"No." Lottie set her candle on an old wooden packing case that seemed to be Sally's bedside table. "Can I sit down?" she asked, waving at the bed.

Sally's mouth worked, as though she wanted to

say no, but in the end she shrugged crossly and moved up. "You can't stay for long. What if the missis comes up here?"

"Miss Minchin? Does she?"

"She might. What are you here for, miss? What do you want?"

"I tried to talk to you before – I've been trying for days. Have you been avoiding me? You leave lighting my fire until you're sure I'm not in my room, don't you?"

A mulish look came over the girl's face. "Why ever would I do that, miss?"

"Because you don't want to talk to me. Because I saw you at the procession. And now I've come up here so you have to. I want to talk to you about the Suffragettes."

"Don't know nothing."

"You do!" Lottie cried angrily.

"Shhhhh! Hush, miss, for heaven's sake. You *will* have the missis up here."

"Then tell me," Lottie hissed. "Or I'll shout.

What was that you were wearing, when I saw you at that coronation procession? I saw you taking it off. It was a Suffragette ribbon, wasn't it? Purple and green and white."

Sally shrugged. "Might have been."

"Where did you get it? Did you know about the Suffragettes? How did you? Have you ever been to any meetings, or . . . or whatever they have?"

Sally stared at her.

Lottie flushed and dipped her head. "I just want to know," she murmured. "How else can I find out?"

"Read a newspaper, like the rest of us!"

"But I can't! Don't you see? We aren't allowed – we only read what we're given. Books for school – even if someone sends one of the girls a novel, she has to show it to Miss Minchin to make sure there's nothing – *you know* – improper."

Sally snorted, and Lottie decided that meant yes.

"We only go out on walks with Miss Minchin and Miss Amelia. When am I supposed to buy a newspaper? Please tell me, Sally. Where did you get the ribbon?"

"I bought it. On one of me afternoons off. I went to the shop."

"There's a Suffragette shop?" Lottie squeaked. "An actual shop you can buy things in?"

"'Course there is. More than one. WSPU shops." She saw Lottie's confused frown and sighed elaborately, obviously enjoying the chance to be superior. "The Women's Social and Political Union. Suffragettes. I goes to the shop in Kensington. In Church Street. They sell all sorts – most of it too expensive for the likes of me. Books, a lot of books. China – like pretty tea sets, in the colours. Jewellery, even. Posters. . ." She darted a sideways glance at Lottie. "Here." She crawled over the narrow mattress and reached down the side where the bed-frame was pushed up against the wall. "I has to keep it hidden, in case someone comes up here nosing." She looked back, smirking a little at Lottie. "Like you."

"I won't tell," Lottie promised eagerly. "What is it?"

"Took a lot of my wages, this did," Sally said, her face taking on an almost reverent look. She drew out a long roll of paper and laid it on the bed between them, unrolling it so that Lottie could see it was a poster, which more than covered the narrow bed.

A girl was standing in a grey doorway, wrapped in a checked shawl that was drawn over her head instead of a coat and hat, her face pale and pinched with cold. She was staring at a sign that said, *Factory Acts Regulations for Women*, and underneath her was written, *They have a cheek. I've never been asked.*

Lottie examined the poster, not wanting to say to Sally that she didn't understand what it meant.

"You're supposed to put them up for people to see." Sally stroked the paper lovingly. "But I can't. Can you imagine the missis if I put it up in the schoolroom?" She snorted.

"I don't know if any of the girls would know what it means," Lottie said slowly.

Sally looked round at her, her eyes narrowing. "You mean you don't?"

"Not properly," Lottie admitted. "I'm sorry. I wish I did," she assured the older girl. "Can't you explain it to me?"

Sally eyed her, half-incredulous. "I suppose. But . . . well. All right. She's a factory worker – maybe a weaver, I don't know. And she's looking at the poster about these new laws that are meant to be about protecting her, but no one ever asked her what the laws should be. What she needs protecting *from*. Because laws are made in parliament and women don't get to vote for who's in parliament. You see?"

"Yes." Lottie nodded humbly. "Does everybody know this sort of thing?" she asked, pleating Sally's thin blanket between her fingers. "I feel like I should too."

"You should. But it isn't your fault. I never

knew much about it while I was at Barkingside. The Girls' Village, I mean. Here. Get up a minute."

Lottie scrambled off the bed and watched, surprised, as Sally rooted under the mattress. She drew out a thin newspaper and handed it to Lottie.

"There. You can borrow it."

Lottie read the cover. "*Votes for Women*. Do you buy this every week?"

"Most weeks, if I can. Depends if I can get to the shop. Sometimes there are lady sellers too."

"On the *street*?" Lottie couldn't keep the shock out of her voice.

Sally nodded. "I couldn't do it. The things you hear people say." She shuddered. "The lady who stands outside the ABC tea shop – men walk past her and whisper swear words, and other things. Things you're too young to hear about." She lifted her nose in the air and looked down it at Lottie.

Lottie sniffed. She didn't really know what

Sally meant, but she wasn't going to let on. "Who is under sentence of death?" she asked, looking at heavy black headline of the newspaper.

"Mrs Napolitano. She killed her husband because he kept hurting her – he even stabbed her nine times, with a knife! The courts say that don't make no difference. The WSPU's campaigning for her to be reprieved."

"But if she killed someone," Lottie tried to argue.

"To stop him killing her! She was defending herself."

"I suppose..." Lottie peered a little worriedly at the small print of the paper. It looked difficult. But clearly Sally was able to read it. "Thank you for letting me borrow this. I . . . I could help you pay for it? I have pocket money."

Sally's face hardened. "I can pay for it myself."

"I didn't mean to say you couldn't – I only wanted to help."

"It's mine. I don't have much, but I have this. You better look after it," Sally added, her brows drawing together in a surly frown. "I want it back."

Lottie sat curled up in bed, holding the newspaper as close as she could to her oil lamp. Although the seminary had gas lighting, it was only in the main rooms and the corridors. The pupils still had to rely on lamps. She was determined to read all of the paper. Even just the bit that she'd read so far seemed to be storing itself up inside her. There was a sort of warm glow in her chest, an angry little fire that she was feeding. It had been lit first by her father's dismissive comments in the letter about her birthday. She had been so hurt by his refusal to visit that she had wanted to do anything, anything to spite him. She had been curious before about Sally and her ribbon, but she might not have done anything about it if it hadn't been for the letter – and perhaps the procession too. The plaintive music and the solemn, determined faces of the marching women had pulled at something inside her. She couldn't forget.

Paying Papa back wasn't a very worthy reason to start supporting the cause, Lottie realized. But surely that didn't really matter? "My birthday money," she whispered to herself suddenly, looking at an advertisement for soap. The paper had advertisements all the way through for Votes for Women tea and scarves and ribbons. "Papa said to buy myself some pretty trinket, so I will. Sally said that the shop had jewellery. Papa's money can go to the Suffragettes, even if I can't do anything else."

Miss Amelia came out of Miss Minchin's sitting room, drawing on her gloves. She smiled at Lottie, and Lottie smiled back, relieved that Miss Minchin hadn't decided to come herself. "Have you decided where you would like to go to buy your present, Lottie? Perhaps Selfridges – such a lovely grand place. A little far, but we could take a cab. Your father has been most generous."

Lottie tried not to wrinkle her nose. Miss Minchin and Miss Amelia had interpreted her father's instructions on a suitable gift for a young lady as a new work box. It was an expensive present, quite clearly, made of walnut and stocked with embroidery threads and all sorts of ribbons and gewgaws, as well as pretty silver scissors, and a strawberry pincushion. Lottie couldn't think of anything she would have liked less. She intended to spend the smaller amount of money he had sent for her own shopping not quite so suitably.

"Could we go for a walk along Church Street, Miss Amelia? There are lots of very pretty shops there. I'd like to look in the windows – I really don't know what I want to buy."

Miss Amelia deflated slightly – she had clearly been looking forward to some more exciting and luxurious shopping – but she nodded. "Of course, dear. You're quite right, I'm sure we will find something there. We'll still take a cab, I think, it must be quite half an hour's walk."

Sitting in the cab, Lottie eyed Miss Amelia from under her hat. She was considerably less frightening than her older sister – so much so that the older girls hardly listened to her at all. Looking at her, Lottie couldn't help wondering if she actually enjoyed being at the seminary. Perhaps she would prefer to have married and had children of her own? Or, given how excited she was about shopping, perhaps she would have liked to own a little shop? A hat shop. Lottie smiled to herself.

"You look happy, Lottie." Miss Amelia patted her hand. "Are you planning your purchases?"

Lottie nodded. "Miss Amelia, one of the other girls told me that there is a WSPU shop in Church Street." It was true – Sally was a girl, after all. Lottie smiled hopefully at Miss Amelia. She might as well sound her out. Miss Amelia might need some softening up to the idea.

"WSPU?" Miss Amelia faltered.

"Yes. The Women's Social and Political Union shop. I was told it has some very fashionable scarves, and even jewellery. I thought I might look there for a present. Would you mind?"

"I don't know, Lottie. I'm not sure if that would be appropriate... The Suffragettes have behaved in the most shocking way – they keep shrieking at dear Mr Asquith, the prime minister, you know, and they are always doing the strangest things, chaining themselves to railings and getting arrested. I really don't think we can allow ourselves to be associated with women such as Mrs Pankhurst and her daughters – they're so . . . so dramatic."

Miss Amelia sounded almost wistful, Lottie thought. She meant dramatic to be an insult, but there was a deeper longing in her voice. She'd had the least dramatic life of anyone.

"Oh, please, Miss Amelia. I only want to look for a scarf. Or perhaps a brooch, or maybe a bag. What do you think? Should I buy a brooch?" Lottie opened her eyes wide, and gazed up at Miss Amelia innocently.

"I suppose the colours are very pretty," Miss Amelia murmured. "I do love purple..."

"Oh, yes," Lottie agreed, trying to keep too much excitement out of her voice as her thoughts tumbled and whirred. Miss Amelia knew the Suffragette colours, then. She was definitely interested – just a little. "And it's so pretty with green. Like flowers, I think. I do hope the jewellery won't be too expensive, Miss Amelia."

Miss Amelia looked out of the smeared window of the cab and nibbled at her bottom lip. "Your father has sent you plenty of money," she murmured at last. "You needn't worry about that."

Lottie squeezed her hands together, trying not to smile too widely.

They left the cab at the end of the street and walked slowly along, admiring the shop windows. Lottie coveted a pair of dancing slippers, rose pink with silver bows on the front. She had to tell herself firmly that she was only looking to throw Miss Amelia off the scent. She didn't want them – even though they were so pretty, and her old dancing shoes were faded... How would Papa ever know what she had bought anyway?

"Would you like to go in and enquire about the slippers, Lottie?" Miss Amelia encouraged.

"No. . ." Lottie said reluctantly. "No, I think not. After all, they'd have to make them to fit and I want to be able to take my present home *today*, Miss Amelia."

"Of course, dear." Miss Amelia sounded as though she was smiling, and Lottie pressed her lips together as she took one last look at the slippers. It had been a silly, spoiled child's thing to say, but still. Everyone insisted on treating her as though she was a baby, someone who couldn't possibly understand anything. She might as well make use of that.

As they were looking into the front of a stationer's, Lottie noticed that the WSPU shop was just a little further down the street. She could see the painted words Votes for Women above the windows. She strolled on as aimlessly as she could, pausing a moment to glance at the pharmacist's display of fancy soaps, and then stopped in front of the windows she wanted. They were so full of posters and newspaper cuttings that it was hard to see inside. Lottie shuddered, her eyes caught by an image of a woman being held down by prison wardresses, while a doctor forced a tube into her throat. Sally's paper had mentioned the heroic women recently released from prison, and that many of them had been forcibly fed, but Lottie hadn't properly understood, she hadn't imagined it like *that*. The woman was fighting – struggling so hard that she had kicked off her shoes – and one of the wardresses was tying her legs to the chair.

Lottie stepped back, almost turning to hurry down the street to Miss Amelia, but then the door of the shop opened and a woman came out, a neat parcel in her hand. She nodded and smiled at Lottie, and Lottie noticed the enamel brooch on the lapel of her jacket – a flag in purple, white and green.

She smiled back a little shakily and peered

through the window at the display behind the posters. It was an odd mixture. Jars of homemade jam were piled up next to books and pamphlets and boxes of tea. There were even board games, something a little like Snakes and Ladders, Lottie thought, trying to get a proper look at the squares on the Pank-a-Squith board.

"There you are, Lottie!" Miss Amelia hurried up, out of breath.

"I was just looking in the windows, Miss Amelia. May we go in?"

Miss Amelia looked around the street nervously, and Lottie understood that she didn't want anyone who knew her to see her going into the shop. "Very well," she whispered, darting forward and struggling with the door. "Oh! Goodness!" She scrabbled at the handle, her eyes watering.

"You need to pull it," Lottie said, gently shooing Miss Amelia inside. She seemed to calm down a little once she was out of sight of the street, blinking in the cool dimness of the shop.

"Good morning," called the woman behind the counter, smiling at them, and Lottie smiled and greeted her back, since Miss Amelia was still snuffling and red-eyed, like a rabbit.

"Look at this pretty blouse," she murmured, lifting the lacy cuff to show Miss Amelia. She'd only been saying it to distract her, but the blouse *was* very pretty, all frills, just the sort of thing Miss Amelia liked. It was also rather oddly normal.

"Is it . . . does it say on it. . ." Miss Amelia whispered, eyeing the blouse fearfully.

"No, I don't think it says 'Votes for Women' anywhere. It's just a nice blouse."

Lottie left Miss Amelia admiring the lace and went to look at a tray of badges. There were enamel flags like the one the lady she'd seen earlier had been wearing, but she couldn't buy anything like that – not to wear at the seminary. Even though Sally had told her that the shops sold all sorts of things, Lottie was surprised at some of the items for sale. She wasn't sure who would want to buy their children a purple and green Suffragette kite.

"Are you looking for anything in particular?" The lady behind the counter was leaning over and smiling at Lottie.

"I wondered, do you have any brooches?" Lottie asked hopefully. "I have some birthday money. . ."

The shop assistant lifted out a tray from under the counter, full of glittering jewellery set against dark red velvet. "Something like this?" she suggested, showing Lottie an amethyst brooch, glowing purple, and surrounded by tiny white seed pearls and a band of green enamel. "One of the local jewellers makes us a selection. I can tell you where the shop is, if you don't see anything you like here."

"That brooch is very pretty, Lottie," Miss Amelia murmured. The charm of the lacy blouse had worn off and she kept glancing worriedly at the windows, as though she expected to see her sister sailing by. "Choose quickly, dear. We should get back."

Lottie nodded. "May I have this, please? Do I have enough?" She still didn't know exactly how much Papa had sent for her, but it must have been quite a lot, judging by the work box. He seemed to be happy to pay to keep her out of his way.

Miss Amelia dug around in her bag for the money, almost dropping the change in her nervousness. "There! Give it to me to put away safely, Lottie." She tucked the little leather box into her bag. "Now we really must go. Good morning," she said firmly to the assistant, ushering Lottie out in front of her. As they hurried up the street, she kept looking behind her, as if the lady from the shop might be chasing after them, shouting something incriminating.

"Sally! Sally, look!" Lottie beckoned, hissing at Sally from her bedroom door. "Come and see."

Sally glanced round shiftily – so much like Miss Amelia that morning that Lottie pressed her hand to her mouth to hide her laugh. The maid hurried over to her, dusting her hands on her apron.

"What? I got fires to do."

"I went to the shop – I spent the money Papa sent me for my birthday." Lottie held out the little box, the brooch sparkling in the evening sun that streamed through the landing window. "He would be furious if he knew. Isn't it funny?"

Sally nodded. "I got to go, miss. I got a lot to do." She went back to pick up her coal box, and Lottie stared after her. "Sally, wait!" She darted out of her room, not caring if anyone saw her talking to the scullery maid. "Don't you see? It's a Suffragette brooch. I read the paper! I bought it at the WSPU shop – Papa's money's gone to the WSPU."

"Money!" Sally muttered scornfully.

"What? That's why they *have* the shops, so people buy things in them. Why are you being like that about it?"

"He'd be furious if he knew," Sally mimicked,

raising her voice and affecting a *la-di-da* accent that Lottie realized was meant to be her.

"Don't!" she whispered furiously. "You're being horrible. And I don't see why!"

"Because he *doesn't* know, does he, miss? You won't tell him. His darling daughter mixed up with the likes of those ugly Suffragettes."

"Well, you don't tell anybody either," Lottie snapped. "You've got that poster hidden under your bed."

"Because I'd lose my place if anyone found out!"

"And I'd get into trouble with Miss Minchin, let alone what she'd say to my father." Lottie sighed, hearing herself. "I suppose it isn't the same."

Sally picked up the box and smiled at her. "Nice pin, though, miss. Pretty."

Chapter Five

Even though Sally had been dismissive, Lottie loved her brooch. It was her own secret rebellion, against her father, against Miss Minchin, against the other girls chattering on about ribbons and hats. It looked so innocent, sparkling at the frilled neckline of her dresses, but it was a hidden message, whispering to Lottie that somewhere, one day, she might belong.

Every week, Lottie would creep up to Sally's attic and borrow the latest edition of *Votes for Women*. She read it cover to cover, shuddering at the descriptions of prison stays and puzzling out the meaning of the cartoons. Some things she didn't understand, however many times she read them, and she would save them up to ask Sally in whispered encounters on the stairs or as they laid the fire in Lottie's room together. Half the time Sally didn't understand them either, but there was no one else they could ask. As the months wore on, and summer turned to autumn, and then freezing fogs began to descend upon the city, the news grew more and more dramatic. Instead of processions and demonstrations, Suffragettes had started to burn postboxes and cut telegraph wires.

Lottie and Sally curled up on the bed in the attic, poring over the descriptions in *Votes for Women*.

"People will be angry," Sally muttered, whistling through her teeth as they read the article. "This is a lot more than marching and making speeches."

"Maybe that's why they're doing it?" Lottie suggested. "If making speeches didn't work.

Perhaps – perhaps people only listen if you break things."

Sally stared at her. "I thought you were meant to be a nice little girl."

"So are most of the Suffragettes. They're ladies, I mean. Mrs Pankhurst and her daughters, they're quite rich, I think." Lottie shrugged. "It's a lot easier to go out protesting and chaining yourself to railings if you don't have to work, isn't it?" She saw Sally's shoulders droop, and thought about what she had said. Even though they were sitting shoulder to shoulder on the bed, there was suddenly a huge gap between them, and Lottie flushed scarlet.

"Maybe not," she whispered sadly. "Maybe it won't be like that, and it's for everyone. I don't know."

"It's disgusting," Jessie hissed, and a hush fell over the dining room. She was at the top of the table, where the older girls always sat.

"I don't believe it," one of the others said, leaning over to look at the letter next to Jessie's toast plate.

"What is it, Jessie?" Lottie called. She didn't care if Jessie was rude to her – it was worth being snubbed, just to find out what was making her so cross.

Jessie peered down to Lottie's end of the table. "What on earth do you want to know for?" she snapped. Then she seemed to relent. Clearly the story was good enough to be worth telling, even to Lottie. "It's a letter from Lavinia, about a wedding."

"A wedding? Is Lavinia married?" one of the littlest girls squeaked, round-eyed with excitement.

"No, of course not!" Jessie sighed, and rested her forehead on her hand – clearly worn out by dealing with these idiotic children. "It's nothing to do with Lavinia – she only met the woman once, she says, and then she read about the wedding in the newspapers. Some ridiculous Suffragette. She refused to make the proper wedding vows and she wouldn't let her father give her away. She wouldn't say that she'd obey her husband. Can you imagine?" Jessie tittered disgustedly. "Ugh, it just shows."

"Just shows what?" Lottie asked. She'd heard the odd comment about Suffragettes from the other girls at Miss Minchin's, but she'd never dared ask any of her schoolmates what they really thought.

"Well, clearly the woman is mad," Jessie pronounced haughtily. "They all are, of course. And completely unwomanly. How could her husband let her behave in such an awful way?" She shuddered dramatically and went back to reading the letter, with the girls on either side of her reading avidly over her shoulders.

Lottie took a bite of toast, chewing thoughtfully. She couldn't imagine being married. Several of the older ones – Jessie included – sighed over the dancing master and his golden hair, but Lottie thought that he was greasy. She imagined Jessie in a white dress, simpering at Monsieur Carle and promising to love, honour and obey. Once she did, she would belong to him entirely, Lottie mused, squashing the crust into her mouth. So would everything she owned, and even her children. A Suffragette wedding sounded perfectly sensible to her.

One afternoon in March, Sally came into the schoolroom to build up the fire. She swept the ashes with a wild banging of the brush across the hearth and clattered the coal. Several of the girls glanced towards her distastefully and tutted. Lottie, who had been sitting talking to Louisa, looked at Sally in surprise. She was perfectly capable of cleaning the hearth in silence, so why was she making such a fuss about it?

Sally caught her eye and jerked her head sideways to the door. Lottie felt her heart beat faster. Something had happened. She carried on listening to Louisa complain about the meanness of Miss Minchin. "And I was not looking over Ermie's shoulder in the history lesson. I mean, why would I, when everyone knows she's a perfect dunce? – I'm sorry, Ermie, but it's true – she was just being an old cat, like always, and it really isn't fair. . ."

"It isn't," Lottie agreed. "Louisa, you've just reminded me, Miss Amelia told me I must mend the flounce on my pink frock before dancing, she'll probably tell Miss Minchin if I don't get it done. I'd better run upstairs and fetch it."

She left Louisa muttering to anyone who would listen, and darted into the hallway, wondering where Sally would have gone after the schoolroom. Perhaps the salon, where dancing would be? The fire in there would need to be built up. She peered round the door, and then sped in, seeing Sally warming her greyed hands at the fire.

"What is it? What was that look for?"

"You'll never guess." Sally's face was alight with news. "They smashed up Pontings!"

"Pontings?" Lottie frowned – it sounded familiar. "Oh! That shop in Kensington High Street." Miss

Amelia had taken her there to choose fabrics for her dresses.

"Drapers – dress fabrics and ribbons and all that." Sally nodded. "They smashed the windows, every one. Great huge cracks in them, Mary said."

"Suffragettes?" Lottie whispered.

"Who else?" Sally muttered scornfully. "You're right, you know. What you said months back. People only listen if you break things up."

"Maybe." Lottie thought of the pretty shop and all the girls who worked there. How must they have felt, seeing stones smash into their windows?

"They did a whole load, all over London, couple of days ago," Sally went on. "All the big shops down Oxford Street. Three hundred Suffragettes, Lottie." Then she sat back on her heels and started to laugh. "And you'll never guess what some of them used to break the glass."

Lottie stared at her. "Stones, I suppose."

Sally shook her head, still giggling. "Toffee hammers! You know, those little hammers you use to break up blocks of toffee. The police said so – it's in Cook's paper. I mean, some stones too. But they say a smartly-dressed lady went to a shop and bought twenty-four toffee hammers, last month. Maybe she didn't know where else to buy a hammer? They must have been planning this for ages."

Lottie shook her head disbelievingly. "I wonder what she said she wanted them for." She started to giggle too. "That's an awful lot of toffee."

"Lottie!"

The two girls whirled round, Sally half-falling backwards to the floor and spilling the coal out of the scuttle. Automatically, Lottie started to help her pick it up, snatching at a piece of coal rolling by her foot, but a disapproving hiss from Miss Minchin made her drop it again. "What do you think you're doing? Come out of here at once. Sally, hurry up and finish your work. I will speak to you later."

Miss Minchin caught Lottie by the wrist and hustled her out of the salon and across the hallway to her own sitting room. It was a dark sort of room, with heavy padded armchairs and a black marble fireplace. "Do you have a taste for low company, Lottie?" she snapped. "Do I need to write to your father and tell him that? What on earth were you doing, sitting there laughing with the scullery maid, as if you were friends? Well? Answer me at once!"

"I . . . I— " Lottie wanted to snap that Sally *was* her friend, more than any of the other girls at the seminary, even Ermengarde. Almost more her friend than Sara was. She and Sally saw each other every day, they talked together, they shared ideas. She only saw Sara every week or so, and Sara had always been more like a loving older sister than a friend her own age.

But if she let out how much time she had been spending with Sally, the maid would probably lose her place. Would she be sent back to the Girls' Village? Lottie wasn't really sure. She would certainly be in disgrace – even more so than she was already. "I was looking for the sash to my dancing dress," she lied, stumbling over the words. "I thought I might have left it in the salon after our last dancing class. That's all."

"Nonsense, you were clearly talking to the maid."

"I only asked her if she'd seen my sash." Lottie widened her eyes and gazed innocently up at Miss Minchin. "I don't know where it is, Miss Minchin, and it's my best blue one. It came undone and I don't want to have lost it."

Miss Minchin glared at her. "I shall be keeping my eye on you, Lottie. Your father has entrusted you to my care. He would not be at all happy to find out that you were hobnobbing with the servants."

"No, Miss Minchin," Lottie agreed. "Shall I go and ask Miss Amelia about my sash? Perhaps she's seen it?"

"Go," Miss Minchin snapped. "Be quick about it."

Lottie hurried down the hallway to the stairs. When she glanced back from the landing, she saw that Miss Minchin was standing in the hall watching her, but in the doorway behind the mistress was Sally, smiling.

"I wish I could do something too," Lottie murmured, throwing *The Suffragette* newspaper on to Sally's bed and marching up and down the tiny attic room.

Lottie's twelfth birthday had passed much like her eleventh, with gifts from her father chosen by Miss Minchin and Miss Amelia. Lottie had not even asked him to visit her this time. Sara had given her a beautiful bracelet, but Lottie far preferred the green, white and purple rosette that Sally had handed to her so shyly, digging it out of her apron pocket on the stairs. She knew how much Sally must have saved to buy it.

"I'm thirteen next month. You were only twelve when you started working here. I hate being shut up at school and taught French and dancing and never anything the least bit useful."

"At least I taught you how to lay a fire. Sit down, Lottie, you're making me tired, striding about like that. I was up before six." Sally swallowed a massive yawn.

"It's nearly two years that I've known about the WSPU, and all I've ever done is read a newspaper and give my pocket money to collections. And even *that* you have to do for me, because I'm never allowed out alone. There are women doing amazing things. Don't you think I could do something for the cause? If I was careful?" Lottie pleaded. "We could at least sneak out and go to a meeting, couldn't we?"

Sally laughed. "Of course you couldn't! Only time I get's my afternoon off. You couldn't come out with me then, you'd be missed at tea. If Miss Minchin or Miss Amelia didn't catch you, one of the other girls would let on. You'd never get away with it."

Lottie slumped back on to the bed. "And what if I didn't get away with it?" she said quietly. "What if I got caught? What would happen?"

"Miss Minchin would write to your father, I suppose. He'd be furious – like you said. That was why you started all this, wasn't it? You wanted to put one over on him."

"That was only how it started," Lottie said swiftly. "It means so much more than that now." Then she added, without looking at Sally, "But if I made him angry, at least he'd be thinking about me."

Sally clicked her tongue. "You want him to come to London and shout at you? What good would that do? What if he takes you back to your great big palace of a house, where you won't even be allowed to go out of the grounds? How'd you get the newspaper, then? You'd be worse off, not better."

"And I'd never see you either," Lottie agreed. "I suppose you're right. Then we'd just better not get caught."

It was easy to say, but Sally was right. Lottie couldn't sneak out to a Suffragette meeting, she was far too closely watched. The only time she was free was now, when all the girls were supposed to be asleep.

I was up before six.

Or early in the morning, before the rest of the house was awake. When Sally went downstairs to light the kitchen stove and get everything ready for when Cook came down.

"Is the door that leads out to the area steps locked at night?" Lottie asked suddenly.

"Of course it is – but the key's on a hook next to it. Why?"

"So we could get out!" Lottie's eyes had brightened. "I was thinking that we'd never be able to, because Miss Minchin keeps the key to the front door, but of course there's the kitchen door as well. I'd never thought of that! Early in the morning, Sally, before everyone else is up – you're up then, anyway, and you could wake me, couldn't you?"

"And what are we going to do, once we're out

of the kitchen door at six in the morning?" Sally asked, frowning.

"I don't know yet." Lottie sighed. "There must be something."

"I'm not breaking windows," Sally said flatly. "Or setting anything on fire. Burning down that church – that was wrong. I'm not even setting a postbox on fire, I don't see why that helps anybody."

Lottie leaned against the wall, gazing at the sloping ceiling. "I know, but . . . if no one listens any other way, maybe it's right," she murmured. "It's a war, Mrs Pankhurst keeps saying so in all her speeches. Suffragettes have to use the weapons of war. They blew up the Chancellor of the Exchequer's house! With a bomb, like real soldiers. If a man did that, he'd be a hero."

"I don't see why putting a bomb in a half-built house makes you a hero," Sally said stubbornly. "At least it was empty. How can Suffragettes be heroes if hundreds of people who had nothing to do with the cause get hurt! They put bombs in that theatre in Dublin last year too, Lottie, a packed theatre. Just because they wanted to catch the prime minister. I don't like him either, but I don't think anyone should be trying to kill him – and what about the people in the audience? They never did nothing wrong!"

"Are you giving up?" Lottie demanded.

"No … I still think women should have the vote – but not like this. You said people only listened when things got broken. I don't want to win like that. And I don't think it'll work either."

"Women have been asking for the vote for years and years, campaigning and writing and making speeches. No one listened! They're listening now, aren't they? *Deeds not Words*."

Sally shook her head. "No. They think all Suffragettes are violent and mad. No one's listening to the words at all, Lottie, they're just angry. Frightened."

Lottie sighed. "I'd just like to do something, like Miss Spark and Mrs Shaw, capturing the

Monument. They didn't hurt anyone, only flew the WSPU colours off the flagpole. Hundreds of people came and watched. It was in all the papers. People *noticed*."

"What are you going to do, take over the Albert Hall?"

"There must be something," Lottie murmured. "Would you write on the pavement?"

"Write what?"

"'Votes for Women'? Maybe some of the other slogans we've seen in *The Suffragette*. In chalk."

"Like they advertise the meetings in chalk messages?" Sally nodded. "That can't hurt anyone. If we're careful, I suppose. I can't lose my place, Lottie. I don't want to go back to the Girls' Village – and I don't know if they'd even take me, now I'm not far off fourteen. If Miss Minchin sends me away and she don't give me a reference, I won't have anywhere to go."

"Maybe you'd better not, it's too risky. But I could do it."

Sally stared at her hands for a moment. "No. You're right. We should do something real. Is there coloured chalk in the schoolroom?"

Lottie nodded. "I'll find some tomorrow in the cupboard. The day after, then?"

"Where are we going to do it?" Sally asked. "It'll have to be somewhere close, if we're to get back before we're missed."

"Here! It's perfect. Anyone who walks past will notice, because they can see from the sign outside that this is a girls' school. It'll be funny. And just think how furious Miss Minchin will be."

"So I'm spending all that time on my knees chalking messages on the pavement just so's the missis can make me wash them off again."

"Oh. I didn't think of that." Lottie's shoulders slumped, and Sally hugged her.

"I'll still do it, silly. Find the chalk, and the day after tomorrow I'll wake you early."

*

"Lottie."

Lottie blinked, the smiling dream of her mother fading away.

"Lottie, it's time. You coming?"

She stared at Sally in the half-light of the morning, and the older girl sighed.

"Wake up. You told me to wake you, remember? Hurry, Lottie, we ain't got long."

Lottie sat up in a rush and flung off her blankets, scrambling out of bed and grabbing for her dress and petticoats. "Wait, wait. I won't be a minute."

Her heart was thumping and her fingers kept slipping on the mother-of-pearl buttons down the front of her dress.

"Here, give me that." Sally took over, buttoning swiftly, and Lottie sighed. "Aren't you nervous at all?"

"'Course I am. I just want to get it done. Come on."

Sally led them down the stairs and through the green baize door into the kitchens, which were dark and smelled of cabbage and burned grease. Lottie shuddered, still half-asleep, and as Sally unhooked the key and started up the area steps to the street, she started to feel sick. She clenched her fingers around the sticks of chalk in her pocket and felt one of them snap.

"Here?" Sally whispered, as they stood by the steps leading up to the grand front door.

Lottie nodded. "'Votes for Women', really big. And then 'Deeds not Words' underneath."

"All right." Sally flinched as a milk cart rattled by and the driver peered at them curiously. "We need to keep an ear out. There might be more deliveries. Or servants who live out walking to work, even. We can't get caught."

"I know. I promise we won't. And if we do," Lottie added suddenly, "you can pretend that you caught me first. I don't care what Miss Minchin does."

Sally laughed, but she sounded too scared for it to be really funny. They crouched down and started to draw out the letters, bumping the chalk over the rough stones of the pavement.

"It's harder than I thought it would be," Sally muttered. "The ground's bumpy. There's hardly any of this piece left. Most of it's all over my fingers. Are we going to have enough?"

Lottie shook her head. "Stick to 'Votes for Women'. There, look. That's all of it written. We just need to fill it in better. Oh! It's all over your dress!" Lottie stood up and tried to brush the chalk dust off Sally's black frock.

"I thought my apron would cover it." Sally rubbed frantically at the dusty cotton. "Cook'll see!"

"She won't, we'll get it off." Lottie swiped at the fabric, but the chalk only seemed to be spreading itself around.

"What you doing?"

Both girls whipped round, panic in their faces. They'd forgotten to keep an eye out for passers-by and two boys were standing behind them, smirking.

"'Votes for Women', eh? Suffragettes, are you?" They were scruffily dressed and Lottie guessed that they were shop boys or apprentices on their way to work.

"Yes," she said, raising her chin. "What's it to you, anyway?"

"Bunch of old cats. You're too young and pretty to be one of them, sweetheart. Here, give us a kiss." The boy slipped his arm around Lottie's waist and she squeaked with horror, wrenching her face away from his. She hardly knew any young men – only Sara's friends, the boys from the Carmichael family who lived across the square, and she was sure none of them had ever even thought of trying to kiss her.

"Get off her!" Sally hissed, trying to grab his arm, but he wheeled round, swinging Lottie away, and the other boy pushed Sally against the iron railings, making her gasp as they thudded into her back.

"What do you think you're doing?" A cold,

furious voice cut through Lottie's frightened panting.

"Mind your own business, miss," the boy holding Lottie said carelessly. "Go on."

"Sara!" Lottie gasped, looking over his shoulder.

"Let her go."

"I won't, dirty little Suffragette. She's no better than she should be."

"Miss, get someone from the house," Sally begged. "Knock on the door. Call Miss Minchin."

"No!" Lottie tried hard to kick the boy's shins, but he only laughed at her – until a long, low growl made him turn again, staring properly at Sara this time.

Boris had come up behind her and she had both hands holding tightly to his collar, pulling him back. He was straining against her, his teeth bared, and he looked terrifying. Lottie had never seen him angry – he was the calmest dog, even when the monkey was pulling his tail and grabbing at his ears. All he ever did was lift his lip a little and shake the irritating creature off. Now the hair on his great neck was standing up and Lottie couldn't take her eyes off his teeth – neither could the two boys.

"Here, you hold that beast back," the boy not holding Lottie said nervously. "Don't you let go of his collar. Alfie, come on. That thing's the size of a horse, look at him."

"All right, all right." Alfie pushed Lottie away, quite gently, so that she stumbled towards Sara, and then to hug Sally, who was still standing limply against the railings. "We're going," he told Sara, holding his hands up peaceably. "Don't get any ideas about letting him go, missy."

"You'd better run, then," Sara said. "I can hardly hold him." Boris growled again, harsh as sawing wood, and both boys dashed away around the corner.

Lottie stared silently at Sara, wondering what she was going to say. She could feel Sally shaking against her, and she realized that Sally had never met Sara, only seen her in the street, getting in and out of her beautiful carriage. All Sally could see was a grand lady – Sara was fifteen now and she wore long dresses, and her dark hair coiled around her head. Even dressed plainly to walk with Boris in the early morning, she looked exquisite.

"She won't tell," Lottie murmured to Sally. "She's a friend. Becky, her maid, she spoke to you when you started at Miss Minchin's, remember?"

"Lottie, what were you thinking?" Sara asked urgently. "What would have happened if Miss Minchin or someone else from the seminary had seen you? It's all very well for you, but Sally would have lost her place, I'm sure of that. You'd better scuff this out." She tried to rub at it with the toe of her beautifully fitted boot, but the chalk only smudged a little.

"Don't!" Lottie cried, and then she glanced round anxiously at the house behind them. The other servants would be rising soon – they needed to get back inside before they were caught. "Don't you think we're right?" she whispered hopefully to Sara. Lottie had never spoken to her about the Suffragettes before, but it was hard to believe that someone she loved so much – someone she thought of as so clever – wouldn't agree with them.

"Oh – I don't know. Maybe. But Uncle Tom doesn't, Lottie. I can't talk about it now. Get inside. And ask Miss Minchin if you can come to tea. I'll send a note."

Lottie nodded reluctantly. Sally was still trembling and Lottie took her hand to lead her back down the steps and into the kitchen. Sally seemed to wake up as soon as she saw the kitchen clock. "I've not lit the fire! Cook'll kill me – get out of here, miss."

Lottie swallowed, hurt. Sally never called her "miss" now, not unless they could be overheard. Sally seemed to have pulled away, as if Sara had reminded her of the gulf between them. "Let me help," she pleaded.

"I'll be quicker on my own. Go on, you can't get caught down here."

Lottie crept away, scuttling up the stairs to hide in her room, all the triumph and excitement she'd expected to feel wiped away.

By the time she was waiting in the hallway to be inspected by Miss Amelia before going out to tea, Lottie had recovered a little. Miss Minchin had been told about the chalked message at breakfast, by Mary, who was bringing her toast. The parlour maid was clearly trying not to laugh and Miss Minchin was furious. She swept across to the dining room windows, which looked out on to the street, like the schoolroom, and glared at the pair of little boys who were standing by the chalk sign, sniggering.

"Remove that at once!" she hissed to Mary, but the maid drew herself up very straight and said that she felt it was not her place. She didn't actually say the words, but what she meant was that she was a parlour maid, not a skivvy. "Then send someone else to do it – the girl in the scullery. It must be cleaned away, I have Lady Nugent and her daughter visiting this morning!"

By now all the girls were trying to peer over at the windows to see what was going on, but no one could see out. As soon as Miss Minchin had crumbled her toast to pieces and swept out of the room, the whole upper class dashed to the windows, leaving the babies of the school begging plaintively to be told what the joke was. Lottie realized she had better look too, otherwise it would seem suspicious.

As they watched, Sally came up the area steps, lugging a bucket of soapy water and a scrubbing brush, and Lottie sighed.

Ermengarde turned to look at her. "What is it?"

Lottie shook her head. "Oh . . . I only wish it could stay, that's all." She smiled brightly at Ermie. "Wouldn't you like to see Miss Minchin's face as she tried to explain that to Lady Nugent?" She tried to keep her voice light, but Sally was on her knees scrubbing the pavement, just as she'd said she would be.

She lingered in the dining room, nibbling at a toast crust, until all the others had gone. Then she ran back to the window, heaving the lower half up with a creak. Sally sat back on her heels, wiping her face with a hand coated in greyish suds.

"I'm sorry!" Lottie hissed, glancing quickly down the area steps in case anyone was there to hear.

"What for?" Sally called back. "We showed those two oiks, didn't we?"

"Well, Boris did. . ."

Sally got up, easing her knees straight slowly, and came back through the iron gate. She stood on the steps so she could whisper to Lottie. "Remember the lady I told you about, who sold *Votes for Women* outside the teashop? And the things the men would say to her, about how she was a loose woman and no better than she should be? She just stood there and let them and smiled, as if she was a . . . a princess. I don't care what those boys said, Lottie. We were there. They know we were there. We stood up." She grimaced at the dusty, wet mess on the pavement. "Even if I do have to scrub it away. We stood up."

"Yes." Lottie stretched her hand out of the window and clutched at Sally's. "And we'll do it again?" she whispered hopefully.

"Too right."

Lottie smiled to herself as Miss Amelia scolded her to straighten her hat and tuck up the petticoats that were showing under her skirt. She wasn't seeing Miss Amelia fussing, she was remembering those boys racing away round the corner of the street. She only wished she had a present for Boris. Perhaps Sara would let her feed him a biscuit.

The chalk still showed a little as she hurried along the street to Mr Carrisford's house. The words were gone, but there was a faint pale ghost of something left behind and Lottie's heart glowed.

She was grinning to herself as she rang the bell and Mr Carrisford's servant Ram Dass answered the door.

He bowed politely to her. Lottie nodded back. "Missee Sahib is in the blue drawing room," he murmured, and Lottie raced past him to the stairs.

Sara was curled on the hearth rug like a child, her cheek pillowed against Boris's dappled fur, but she jumped up when Lottie came in. She seized Lottie's hands and gazed into the younger girl's face, her grey eyes worried.

"Lottie, how could you?"

"Oh, don't!" Lottie pulled her hands away. "Don't spoil it."

"*I* spoil it?" Sara looked angrier than Lottie had ever seen her. "How can you say that? What would have happened if I hadn't woken early this morning? If I hadn't decided that it was so beautiful I'd take Boris out for an airing?"

Lottie slumped next to the great dog, who was looking back and forth between them anxiously.

She rubbed her hand round one of his huge silken ears, threading it between her fingers over and over. "I don't know," she admitted. "But we did it, don't you see? It was important."

"What will you do now?" Sara asked quietly, sitting beside her. Boris thumped his heavy tail into the hearth rug twice and settled back down.

"Try and think of other things to do." Lottie glared at her determinedly. "And when I'm older, I don't care what Papa says, I shall join the WSPU and be a proper Suffragette."

Chapter Six

After Sara had rescued them that morning, she seemed to feel responsible for distracting Lottie from the Suffragettes. She invited her to tea almost every week, and kept lending her books. Most of them were rather long, and about history, which was Sara's favourite subject, and Lottie did not read them all, although she tried. She had her own tiny library in her room now, mostly books and pamphlets that she had sent Sally to buy for her from the WSPU shop. They were hidden between the books Sara had lent her, so that Miss Amelia wouldn't see what they were.

Early in June, Miss Minchin called Lottie and Ermengarde to stay behind at the end of morning lessons. This usually meant that whoever she wanted to talk to had done something wrong, but Lottie really couldn't think of anything, for once. She and Ermengarde hadn't been gossiping together. Even her composition had been remarkably free of blots and smears this morning. Ermie had been shamefully forgetful in the French lesson, but then she usually was.

"I have had a note from Miss Crewe, inviting you both to spend the day with her this Saturday." Miss Minchin's lips were pursed, as though she were sucking on a lemon. "I feel it is most inappropriate of her to have asked you, as you will miss your morning's work. But there we are." She sniffed disapprovingly. "I suppose that you would like to go?"

"Yes, Miss Minchin," Ermengarde said politely, and Lottie nodded. "Yes, please."

"Very well. You may both write a polite note to her this afternoon, expressing your pleasure at the invitation."

"Miss Minchin would be even more horrified if she knew where Mr Carrisford was going to take us," Ermengarde whispered to Lottie, as they left the schoolroom. "She told me about it yesterday when I went to tea."

"Where?" Lottie demanded eagerly, pulling Ermengarde up the stairs and out of Miss Minchin's earshot. "What are we going to do?"

"To the races, to watch the Derby. I should think Miss Minchin would say that racing is terribly vulgar, but it can't be, since the king and queen will be there. It's very dressy and sociable, Sara said."

Lottie stared at her. "Really? We're all to go?"

"Yes, and Mr Carrisford told Sara that he will hire a tall carriage, with space on the roof for us to sit and watch. And there will be a picnic, with the most delicious things, and a supper too. We won't get back to school until quite late." Ermengarde sighed delightedly.

"Have you ever been to a horse race before?" Lottie asked curiously.

Ermengarde laughed. "No. It isn't at all the sort of thing that Papa or the aunts would take me to. Museums and picture galleries, that's where they like to drag me. Oh, and events like the Festival for the coronation, because of that awful historical pageant, and all the interesting facts that I could learn about the countries of the Empire. A horse race is much more exciting. There'll be crowds and crowds of people and we will get to see all of it, Lottie."

"And a whole day away from here." Lottie sighed.

Ermengarde stared at her. "Do you really dislike it so much?" she asked.

Lottie shrugged uncomfortably. "I don't know why. I've never known anywhere else, since I can hardly remember living at home. But yes. Maybe I wouldn't be happy anywhere, Ermie.

Perhaps I'm a person who is always destined to be miserable." Lottie sat down on the stairs and sighed mournfully.

Ermengarde sniffed. "If Miss Amelia hears you talking like that, she'll say you're bilious and dose you with Milk of Magnesia."

"Ermengarde St John, you are the least sympathetic person I have ever met," Lottie muttered.

Lottie was sure that she had never seen so many people. They were everywhere, crowding against the barriers, men and women in their best summer clothes, all talking and laughing and shouting. It was almost frightening, to be surrounded by so many, and it reminded her of the crush around the coronation procession, two years ago this same month. Back then, she'd hardly even heard of Suffragettes.

Mr Carrisford had swept up in front of the seminary not in a carriage, as the girls had expected, but in a motorcar, a huge, shining, chauffeur-driven car, with room for all four of them, and several wicker hampers.

"Atkins here knows the very best place for us to watch from," he had assured Lottie and Ermengarde as they climbed in. "By the curve of the track. We shall be there nice and early, and you will have the best of views, I promise. And once we've eaten lunch, you can stand on the hampers too."

Atkins had been quite right – the view from up above the crowd was very clear. On the other side of the course were several men with film cameras, positioned to catch the horses as they came out of the bend.

"The next race is the important one, the Derby itself," Mr Carrisford explained, leaning down to pull Lottie on to the seat of the car so she could see properly. "See, everyone's pushing back towards the rails now. No one wants to miss this."

Lottie peered past the sea of straw boaters and

flowered hats at the course, watching the runners come galloping to the corner. Her heart beat faster as the horses raced towards them, and the crowd roared and shifted and danced.

"Speeding up again now after the bend," Mr Carrisford murmured. Sara clasped her hands excitedly as the first horse dashed past, a clump of others right on its heels.

Lottie heard herself cheering, so wild with the excitement that she hadn't even realized she'd opened her mouth. Sara was pressed against her, shining-eyed. Lottie clapped her hands delightedly, caught in the thundering beauty of the horses.

The shouting checked for a moment, and a strange gasp ran through the crowd. People began to spill out on to the course, running towards a dark mass on the grass. Mr Carrisford leaned forward anxiously. "Did a horse fall? I didn't see, I was looking further down the course. What happened?"

"A lady – she was out on the grass. . ." Lottie

pressed her hand against her lips, sickened by the ragdoll tumbling of that slight figure. "The horse fell over her, the rider came off. . ."

"What was she doing?" Mr Carrisford demanded almost angrily. "It's madness – did she faint and fall under the rails? How can that have happened?"

"I don't know." Lottie slipped down on to the seat, and Sara pressed a bottle of salts into her hand. Lottie sniffed at the glass bottle, gasping, her eyes watering at the acrid scent. Ermengarde was huddled in the side of the car looking horrified. Lottie felt Ermie's cold hand creep into hers. The voices all around them sounded like shrieking birds. Her head whirled, the birds pecking and tearing, and Lottie buried her face in Sara's shoulder with a whimper.

"I can't believe that she would do that. . ." Sally whispered. She had borrowed Cook's copy of the *Daily Sketch*, the front cover a sickening photograph of the fallen horse and the woman who had dashed out in front of him. Her hat was rolling towards the camera.

"How could she? We said we would stand up, but . . . but . . . not like that." The paper shook in Lottie's hands.

"It isn't even the headline. Have you noticed?" Sally asked drearily. "They're more interested in the hundred to one winner. She's *dying*."

"Do you think she is? You don't think she'll get better?"

"It says she's still unconscious. You saw, Lottie, she went under the horse's hooves. No one could survive that, surely."

Lottie shivered, remembering the tumbling body. She couldn't picture Miss Davison ever waking up.

Sally bought newspapers with Lottie's pocket money, and they read them frantically, late at night in the attic, searching for any mention of Miss Davison's health. The papers were full of criticism for the Suffragette's mad act, but there were no updates on her recovery. Then on June 9th, five days after the race, Lottie awoke to find Sally shaking her. The older girl's eyes were red and her face was streaked with tears.

"I can't stay, I'm meant to be down in the kitchen. Cook'll be shouting for me. I went out to get it, Lottie, look." She held up the *Daily Sketch* again, the headline in heavy black letters. *First Martyr for Votes for Women.*

"She's died?" Lottie sat up, taking the newspaper in shaking hands. She had known – almost – but a tiny kernel of hope had been inside her. "A martyr?" she whispered. "They mean – she did it on purpose? She *wanted* to be killed?"

"I don't know – that must be what it means. But some of the other papers said she was trying to stop Anmer because he was the King's horse. To get the attention of the King, for the cause. She tried to grab his bridle." Sally gazed at the headline uncertainly. "Well, you saw her. Do you think she meant to be hit?"

Lottie shook her head. "I couldn't see, it was

so fast. She was just there, and then . . . then she was on the ground and so was the horse, and the jockey." She wrapped her arms around her waist, feeling herself start to shiver.

"Oh, Lottie." Sally sat on the bed next to her and put an arm around her shoulders. "Get up. Go down to breakfast early, have a cup of tea."

"I don't want to. I don't want to have to talk to anyone," Lottie whispered. "Sally, we should do something. We have to. Will there be a march, or a meeting – somewhere people talk about Miss Davison? Can't we go? I'll sneak out, I'll lie and say I'm going to visit Sara. Couldn't we find some sort of excuse for you?"

"There'll be her funeral, I suppose," Sally said doubtfully. "We could go and watch outside, even if we can't go into the church."

"But when will it be? We can't know. Unless they put it in *The Suffragette*." Lottie straightened up, pulling away from Sally a moment. "The shop! They'd know, maybe?"

"I'll go and ask. Cook'll send me out for something or other, she usually does. I'll just go the long way round. I have to get back downstairs, Lottie. Here, you can keep this to read. I won't have time."

Lottie nodded, smoothing the paper over her knees. She still wanted to cry, but at least if they could go to the funeral, they'd be showing that it mattered. "I should think lots of women will come," she whispered to herself.

The shop in Church Street had nothing to tell Sally, but the woman behind the counter had come around the front and hugged her, she told Lottie that night.

"She said I was a darling girl." Sally muttered sadly. "She said she wished all the girls in service were standing up for our rights. She's going to write to you, she promised. As soon as they know anything about the funeral – she was sure that the WSPU would have a plan, probably there'll be a procession. I told her I never got no letters, and Cook would want to know what it was, so she'd better write to you instead." She looked worried for a minute. "I s'pose Miss Minchin's going to know it's not from your father."

"I'll tell her it's from one of my cousins – she doesn't know that I don't have any. It'll be all right, Sally, don't worry. You're a marvel."

Lottie watched eagerly for letters for the next few days, ready with her excuse. Miss Minchin frowned as she dealt out the letters, but the neat little envelope was clearly addressed to Lottie in a curling, ladylike hand. "Lottie?"

Lottie tried to look unconscious. "A letter from Papa?" she asked innocently. "Oh – no. From my cousin Lily, I think. Thank you, Miss Minchin." She strolled away, resisting the urge to rip the envelope apart, and hurried upstairs. Sally must open it – she had made all the effort, after all.

That night she crept out of her room without a candle, as the midsummer night was hardly dark. She padded up the stairs in her slippers and found Sally waiting for her anxiously.

"Did a letter come?"

Lottie held it out, watching eagerly as Sally wrenched at the flap.

"'Dear Miss Lane' – Miss Lane!" Sally blinked. "No one ever calls me that. 'Dear Miss Lane. There is to be a procession across London, accompanying Miss Davison's body to St George's Church, Hart Street, Bloomsbury. Our society has been invited to take part in the procession, and I wondered if you and Miss Legh would like to march with us?'" Sally looked up at Lottie, wide-eyed. "'We will be meeting at the shop at midday, to make sure we can assemble at Buckingham Palace Road in time to march off at two. We will be wearing white dresses, with a two-inch black armband. Purple ribbons, if you have any, would be appropriate. I do hope that you can join us to bid farewell to our dear and brave sister Emily.'" Sally stared at the letter, biting her lip. "I haven't a white dress," she murmured.

"But my dresses would fit you easily and I have several white ones," Lottie pointed out swiftly. "I know you wear long skirts now, but it wouldn't matter, would it? I can lend you good black stockings too. You could wear your own dress over the top and take it off when we get to the shop."

"I never thought she'd remember to write," Sally muttered, looking worriedly at Lottie. "How can I go? Saturday's not my afternoon off."

"You must!" Lottie pleaded. "I won't go without you, oh, Sally, please!" She frowned. "Your lady from the Girls' Village, who comes to check on you. Could you say you have to meet her? We can write – I'll write a letter, saying you must come out to Barkingside on the train, and enclosing money for your ticket! That would give you most of the day, wouldn't it?"

Sally nodded.

"And I shall beg Sara to invite me." Lottie pressed her lips together. "I know Mr Carrisford doesn't approve of Suffragettes, but I shall make her. I will."

*

"I thought you weren't coming," Sally gasped, as Lottie pelted towards her.

"I'm sorry! Miss Minchin watched me walk along to Sara's house, with the most bad-tempered look on her face! I had to go in and then sneak out around the back. Ram Dass showed me out of the kitchens with such a grand bow. I feel sure he was laughing at me inside, but he was so dignified, you'd never have known it."

"Did you tell Miss Sara what you were doing?"

Lottie shook her head. "Not after I'd thought about it. I told Miss Minchin that I was going to Sara's for the day, but I never actually asked Sara. I didn't want her to have to lie to Mr Carrisford, and she might have tried to persuade me out of going. So I just didn't tell her. Ram Dass didn't mind, though. He can't stand Miss Minchin, she draws her skirts in if she passes him in the street, I've seen her do it. He just stands up even straighter and walks like a prince."

"Oh, well. I suppose it's all right, as long as he

isn't going to blab. We'll have to hurry to get to Church Street on time." Sally frowned. "I'm sure it must be late."

"No, it's only a little after eleven, Sally, honestly. And don't worry, I have all the pocket money saved up that we haven't used on newspapers, and I borrowed some more from Ermie in case. Let's just get a little way away from here and we can catch a bus, or even a hansom cab if we have to."

They hurried along the street, Lottie walking backwards half the time to look for buses. "There!" She waved urgently to the driver, who looked for a moment as if he wasn't going to stop for a pair of children, but then pulled in to the side of the road. The girls clambered up the twisting staircase to the roof, and Lottie dug around in her purse for the fares. "I have the black bands, look." She retrieved them from the purse with a jingle of coins. "I cut up one of my wool stockings, do you think they will be neat enough?"

Sally nodded. "Are we really doing this, Lottie?" she asked.

"Yes. We can't turn back now, we'd never be able to explain. We're going."

The bus took them as far as Kensington High Street, and they raced up Church Street, pounding past the shops that Lottie had visited with Miss Amelia two years before. The windows of the WSPU shop were veiled in purple cloth, with a photograph of Emily Wilding Davison on an easel in the middle of one and a wreath placed in front of it. Lottie swallowed hard, seeing for the first time the face of the woman whose body she had watched flung into the air.

The tiny, wedge-shaped shop was packed with women in white dresses, holding flowers and wreaths, and the two girls loitered shyly by the door, until Sally pointed to one of the women, and whispered, "That's her. Miss Bailey, the one who wrote to us."

"Girls – Sally!" The young woman edged her

way through the crowd, holding out her hands to them. "You came – I wasn't sure if you'd be able to get away from the school."

"I do have a white dress, miss," Sally gasped out. "It's on underneath, I couldn't wear it out."

"Clever girl. Here." She led them through to a little storeroom in the back of the shop. "The meeting rooms upstairs are all full of people sorting flowers and banners. Change in there, child."

"I'll wait here for you." Lottie stood in front of the door, watching hungrily as the white-clad women passed by, their arms full of flowers. She turned as the door behind her creaked, and Sally came out of the storeroom, her hair hanging around her shoulders instead of scraped back into a bun, wearing Lottie's best white dress.

"You look younger than me!" Lottie said, surprised.

Sally hunched her shoulder in an awkward shrug. "I'm only a year older. Can't help being short."

"I didn't mean that – I think it's your hair." Lottie had always thought of it as a sort of faded fair colour, tucked away under a cap, but now, streaming loose down Sally's back, there were silvery lights in it and her whole face looked softer. She was wearing her own plain straw hat, but that only made her seem more childlike.

"Oh, well done." Miss Bailey came hurrying past again, and smiled at them. "Here, take these." She pressed a small bunch of lilies into each of the girls' hands. "We'll all be carrying them." She looked at Lottie and Sally, clearly a little embarrassed. "We're planning to take the Underground to St James Park. Do you have money for the fare?"

"Yes, miss." Sally nodded firmly. "We have plenty. Don't worry. Thank you for the flowers, and for letting us come."

"I've never been on the Underground," Lottie whispered to Sally, as Miss Bailey scurried away to give out more flowers.

"Me neither."

Passers-by were staring at them, even as they walked to the Underground station, a group of girls and women dressed all in white and carrying flowers. Lottie tried to walk as though she were marching, and not to look round at the loud comments, but she stood on the Underground platform with her cheeks burning scarlet as two women loudly discussed her age, and how she and Sally were being led astray by "those absurd women". She hung her head, the choking funeral smell of the Madonna lilies reminding her strangely of the dream of her mother. She rubbed her fingers over the stamens, watching the pollen stain her fingers gold.

"Do you feel led astray?" Miss Bailey asked, whispering in her ear.

Lottie shook her head firmly. "If Miss Davison could do . . . what she did, why should we care what they say?" she murmured back.

"It's not absurd, miss. It's grand," Sally added. "We're like a guard of honour, for a dead soldier."

"Exactly." Several of the other women turned to smile at them, and Sally flushed and stared down at her boots.

They had seen the Women's Coronation Procession, two years before, but Lottie had not expected that the funeral procession would be almost as huge. Women in white were everywhere, but there was no hum of chatter, only a deep feeling of grief and determination. They lined up in rows behind the Kensington Society's banner, draped in purple fabric for mourning, and Lottie stood clutching her lilies, feeling tears burn behind her eyes. She was sad – she was crying, there were tears on her cheeks as the music floated back from the brass band ahead of them – but surely it was wrong to feel so happy too? For once, she felt as if she were in the right place, and as they began to march, she was filled with a strange, blissful sense of peace.

By the time they had gone back to the shop for Sally's dress and bundled her hair up under her hat again, it was early evening, more than an hour after they were expected back at Miss Minchin's. As they rounded the corner of the street into the square, Lottie suddenly stopped and thrust Sally behind her. Miss Minchin herself was walking up the street from Mr Carrisford's house, with her best hat on.

"She's been to look for me," Lottie muttered. "She saw us, I think." She glanced at Sally and saw the colour fade out of her face. "Don't worry. Just follow what I say. And walk behind me."

She set her shoulders back and marched round the corner again, to find Miss Minchin almost upon them, her face furious.

"Charlotte Legh! Where have you been? I've just come back from Mr Carrisford's house. Oh, yes – I went to fetch you, and his servants told me that Miss Sara was in her drawing room and you hadn't been there all day. So, where were you, you degenerate child?" She noticed Sally behind Lottie, and gasped with anger. "You too! You were with her? Well, that's simple enough. You will leave at the end of week, when I've found your replacement."

"With *me*?" Lottie glanced disdainfully round at Sally. "She most certainly was not. I met her while I was walking and she insisted on following me."

"I was at Barkingside, ma'am," Sally muttered politely. "I went to visit my house mother. She still writes to me, she asked me to come. It's part of the arrangement with the authorities, ma'am. She has to report on my welfare. I saw the young lady on the way back from the station, and I thought she ought not to be on her own, so I ventured to accompany her, ma'am."

Miss Minchin eyed her narrowly. "Very well. Go on, there will doubtless be duties for you in the kitchen. Hurry along. As for you," she glared at Lottie, "you will come with me." She seized Lottie's arm and marched her back along the road. "Where have you been?" Then she wrenched at the black armband around Lottie's sleeve, almost tearing it off.

"No!" Lottie cried, twisting out of Miss Minchin's grip and trying to cover it up. "No, you mustn't!"

"Ridiculous," Miss Minchin snapped, ripping the band away. "I suppose you sneaked out to go to the funeral for that madwoman."

"She wasn't," Lottie gasped. "How can you call her that?"

"Of course she was – and this funeral procession was a disgusting, sentimental display. Far better for the poor creature to have been buried quietly somewhere, instead of that vulgar show. All she has done is to inspire further criminal acts of deceit from foolish children like you. I shall write to your father tonight, telling him how you have lied and schemed and drawn others into your lies too."

Chapter Seven

Lottie lay curled up at the pillow end of her bed, huddled into a tight ball. She had kicked the covers off long ago, but the June night was hot and it hadn't woken her. She had been dreaming on and off all night, it seemed. She kept being jolted awake by the image of Miss Minchin's white and furious face, or the sickening moment when Miss Davison was hurled through the air. The scent of lilies drifted through the room and she settled again, pulling the sheet around her shoulders. Someone was walking towards her, and Lottie smiled in her sleep, turning to see a figure in a white dress. Her mother stroked her face, murmuring something that Lottie couldn't hear, however hard she tried. She was smiling too, laughing almost, creases at the corners of her eyes, the same round eyes as Lottie's.

Lottie reached out her arms, stretching, hoping for an embrace, but nothing was there. Her fingers closed on empty air, and she opened her eyes, gazing around the room in confusion. What had she been dreaming about? Something good – something happy. But then it had gone. . .

Lottie pulled her dressing gown from the end of her bed and slipped it on. The letter was in the pocket, where she had left it last night, and her fingers shook as she began to unfold the paper.

I have just received a letter from Miss Minchin, as you are no doubt aware. I am enclosing this note for you inside my reply. I have made it clear to Miss Minchin how very concerned I am that you have come into such terrible company, while I had thought you safe and cared for at her seminary. This will not be allowed to happen again.

However, it is clear that lack of supervision by itself could not have brought you to associate with these desperate creatures. There must be something in you that has led you to this. I am ashamed to call you my daughter, and I must warn you that I cannot allow you to ruin our family name any further. If I hear of this kind of behaviour again, I will at once remove you from school.

With forced calm, Lottie refolded the letter and tucked it back into her pocket. She had read the note from her father so many times now, and every reading made her feel sick. She had been so desperate for his attention. She had said that she didn't care if he was angry. She wanted to be taken away from Miss Minchin's, even if she couldn't think of her father's house as home. She had been desperate for him to worry about her. To be on his mind.

Now she could have all of that. Miss Amelia had searched her room and taken away Lottie's copy of Sylvia Pankhurst's book, and all the pamphlets she had been hiding behind Sara's books about history, but it would be easy enough to get Sally to buy her some more. She would only have to show them to the other girls in the schoolroom. She would probably be home in disgrace by the next day.

But the icy disgust in her father's letter chilled her. She kept imagining him saying the words, telling her that there was something inside her that had led her to behave this way, that he was ashamed to call her his daughter. How could he write such things? How could he know anything about her, when he hadn't seen her in so long?

Lottie peered across at the photograph on top of her chest of drawers. It was not very recent, and most of it was a large moustache. She was finding it hard to remember what her father actually looked like. Would she even recognize him, if he walked past her in the street? She had an awful feeling that the answer was no. How could she love him, if he was a stranger? Lottie pressed her hands to her cheeks, her fingers cold with fear. She loved her mother more, and her mother was dead.

Wouldn't it be better to behave? To stay here at Miss Minchin's instead, safe and quiet?

And terribly, dismally enclosed.

"I have discussed your father's letter with Miss Amelia." Miss Minchin's face was still pale, with patches of ugly red across the tops of her cheeks. The letter was open on her mahogany desk and she kept smoothing it out as she spoke to Lottie, as though she couldn't leave it alone. Her father must have written awful things to Miss Minchin too, Lottie realized. He had blamed Miss Minchin and Miss Amelia for letting her fall into bad company. "We are willing to keep you here at the school – for the moment. But only on the understanding – and I shall explain this to your father – that you are not allowed out."

"Not allowed out. . ." Lottie echoed slowly.

"No. Not at all. Oh, you will be able to go on walks with the rest of the girls, but you will walk with Miss Amelia or myself at all times. And that is all. No visits. No little trips to have tea with Miss Crewe next door. Since she has obviously been conspiring in your dreadful lies." Miss Minchin's eyes glittered, and Lottie saw that this was the only part of the situation that made the old woman happy. "I shall, of course, write to her guardian," she said piously. "He must be informed that Miss Crewe has been involved in this behaviour."

Lottie swallowed hard, hoping that Sara's Uncle Tom wouldn't be too angry with her. Sara had said that he didn't approve of Suffragettes. He would probably be furious, Lottie thought miserably. She had got Sara into trouble too.

"Do you realize that you were associating with

hardened criminals at that funeral procession?" Miss Minchin demanded. "Women who have been repeatedly imprisoned, for acts of violence and trespass? Is that where you want to end up, Lottie? In Holloway Prison?"

Lottie shook her head, trying not to shudder. The descriptions of the prison in *The Suffragette* were so frightening, she was not sure she would ever be brave enough to risk being arrested.

"Look." Miss Minchin rustled through a pile of papers on her desk and pulled out a newspaper, folded open to show a page of photographs. "These are convicts. Notorious criminals, pictured here so that the law-abiding public can be wary of them. Women like these burn down houses, Lottie. They attack ministers, smash windows, plant bombs."

Lottie took the paper, gazing at the faces. They had been taken as the women were released from prison, and they looked exhausted, even though some of them were smiling. She traced her fingers across the page, trying to imagine what they were like. Some of the women she had marched with had been to prison. Miss Davison had been in Holloway for six months. She had even tried to jump off a prison balcony to call attention to the way the women were being treated.

The last woman in the line was smiling. Her light hair was curling and tangled around her face, and her coat hung shapeless, as though it no longer fitted properly. But it was the smile that caught Lottie. The way her eyes creased at the corners. Lottie's heart began to bang against her ribs and, for a moment, she was sure she could smell lilies.

"I . . . I didn't think," she whispered. Her voice was shaking, as though she was frightened, and Miss Minchin nodded approvingly.

"This is where these Suffragettes end up. I'm glad to see that you are taking it to heart."

"May I take this away to read?" Lottie asked. If Miss Minchin said no, she was not sure that she would be able to let go of the paper.

"Very well. You will continue to stay in your

bedroom until I have had further discussion with your father. Read that newspaper, and think about the way you have disappointed your father and your schoolmates."

"Yes, Miss Minchin," Lottie murmured, stumbling out of the room.

"Lottie?" Miss Amelia peered nervously around the bedroom door, as if she feared that Lottie had become some sort of wild, frightening creature who might leap at her if she wasn't on her guard.

Lottie pushed herself up on her elbows and looked over at her. She had been lying on her bed for hours, gazing at the newspaper and wondering if she was imagining the likeness to her dream. Not that it really mattered – her mother was dead, so of course this couldn't be a photograph of her. But it was so *like* her. She could keep it to look at it, anyway. She couldn't *stop* looking at it. Her eyes seemed to be pulled back to it every time, as though she was hungering for the sight of it.

"I've brought you some supper." Miss Amelia put the tray on Lottie's desk, and came over to the bed, frowning a little. "Get up and eat, Lottie."

"I'm not hungry," Lottie murmured. She wasn't hungry for food.

"What have you got there?" Miss Amelia reached out for the newspaper, but Lottie snatched it away, scrambling back up the bed, and clutching it tightly against her chest. "No!"

"Lottie, whatever's the matter? It's only a newspaper." Miss Amelia sighed wearily, and sat down at the end of the bed. "I should never have let you go to that shop," she murmured. "It all started there, didn't it? I should have known – it was bound to happen."

Lottie lowered the newspaper a little and eyed her curiously, her breath still coming fast. "What was bound to happen?"

Miss Amelia's eyes widened, and she jumped up hurriedly. "I really don't know what I meant. Nothing. Eat your supper, Lottie."

"No." Lottie ran her fingers through her hair, leaving it standing up in a wild cloud. "What did you mean? That wasn't nothing." She slipped off the bed and followed Miss Amelia, who was standing with her hand on the door handle. "You can't go. You have to tell me."

"Nonsense! I don't have to do anything of the sort," Miss Amelia twittered nervously. "You are a dreadful child, Lottie. You always were, but I suppose it's hardly your fault . . . oh dear. . ."

"Why? Why isn't it my fault?" Lottie demanded, pulling at Miss Amelia's sleeve. Then she frowned. "Miss Amelia, why is my father so ashamed of me? Why doesn't he ever come to see me?"

Miss Amelia's mouth opened and shut, though no words came out. She tried to pull her sleeve away, but Lottie clung on tight.

"If it isn't my fault, whose fault is it?" Lottie stared at Miss Amelia's pink face. "My mother's?" She caught her breath. "Did she fall in love with someone else?"

"Oh, no, nothing like that," Miss Amelia assured her. "If there had been a scandal, my sister would never have taken you as a pupil. She did consider telling your father we couldn't keep you, when he divorced your mother, but there was very little talk, so. . ."

"What?" Lottie squeaked.

"Oh dear. . ." Miss Amelia murmured faintly – but was there a tiny glint of excitement in those faded blue eyes, too? "Lottie, don't be upset. Divorce isn't really such a shameful thing. It happens more and more often these days."

"I don't care about that!" Lottie shook her head, like a horse trying to get rid of flies. "If Papa divorced my mother after I came here, she must still have been alive!"

"Well, yes. . ."

"But she *died*! That's why I was sent to school, because my mother was dead and my father didn't know how to bring up a girl on his own. And now you're telling me she wasn't dead at all." Lottie's eyes widened. "Miss Amelia, when did she die? Did she *ever* die? Are you telling me that she's been alive, all this time?"

"I'm not telling you anything of the sort," Miss Amelia said swiftly. "Nothing. You're making up a great deal of nonsense, Lottie. I shouldn't be surprised if you were coming down with a fever." She wrenched herself away from Lottie at last, and backed out of the door.

"There's all sorts of gossip running round this place," Sally muttered, as she slipped in to see Lottie later that night. "I gave up waiting for you to come upstairs."

Lottie looked up at her vaguely. "I'm sorry. I meant to . . . I just didn't know what to do. I was thinking. What time is it?"

"Late. Nearly midnight. What's the matter? You look half-wild. The state of your hair, it's like you've been poking sticks in it." She settled cross-legged on Lottie's bed. "If anyone comes to check on you,

I'll just have to jump down the other side. I had to come and see if what they're saying downstairs is true. Are you being sent away?" She pleated her nightdress between her fingers, staring down at it fiercely.

Lottie shook her head. "I don't think so. I'm not sure what's going on." She rubbed her reddened eyes with her fists. "Look at this." She thrust the newspaper under Sally's nose and watched her eagerly.

"What am I looking at?" Sally frowned at the photograph. "Suffragettes leaving prison. I don't understand."

"No." Lottie sighed, and took the paper back. "No, you wouldn't. I'm being stupid. I'm making it all up. That's what Miss Amelia said, and it's probably true."

"For pity's sake, Lottie. Start at the beginning. You're making no sense."

"My mother wasn't dead when I was sent to school." Lottie swallowed hard. Saying the words aloud seemed to set them in stone. Everything she knew had been based on a lie.

"Wait, wait a minute. Why'd you get sent away, then? I thought you were supposed to be such a little horror your pa couldn't deal with you on his own?"

"I never said that!" Lottie glared at her.

"Everybody else did."

Lottie sniffed crossly. "That's still what happened. She wasn't dead – she just wasn't there. He divorced her, so I suppose she must have left him."

"You mean she—"

"What?"

"Nothing." Sally looked away uncomfortably, and Lottie nodded.

"Yes, I suppose so. She left me behind."

"Unless he threw her out. He could have done, you know. Any children belong to their father, if he wants them."

"But he didn't want me," Lottie whimpered. "He

sent me *here*! If that's true, it's just that he didn't want her to have me."

"What's all this got to do with this newspaper, anyway?" Sally leaned over to look at it again. Then her eyes widened. "You reckon she's still alive?"

Lottie pointed to the woman on the end. "What if it was all a lie? There's nothing to say she ever really died, is there? I've not seen her in eight years, except in dreams. But this photo – it's so like I remember her. She looks like this when I dream about her, this same smile. I know it sounds unlikely, but I've never seen this picture before, I can't have done. This is yesterday's paper. So how can she be so familiar? What if that's why my father's so furious about me being involved with Suffragettes? What if he thinks I'm taking after my mother?"

"She does look a bit like you." Sally squinted between the photo and Lottie. "Same hair. Big eyes. But lots of people look a bit alike. . ."

"I know." Lottie flopped down on the bed again,

staring miserably at the ceiling. "I could be making up the whole story out of nothing." Then she propped herself on her elbows. "Except I'm not, you know. They did still lie about her being dead. All those people who said I was such a poor little thing, to have a dead mother, how sorry they were for me. They were *all* lying."

"I s'pose he could have told everyone she was dead, if he was that shamed they were living apart," Sally said thoughtfully. "So what are you going to do about it?"

Lottie sighed. "I want to ask my father – but I can't. Miss Minchin's sure to read my letters, and who's to say he'll tell me the truth anyway, when all he's done so far is lie?"

"He must have explained it to Miss Minchin to start with."

"Yes, but she isn't going to tell me."

"I know that," Sally said patiently. "But she has that great desk full of letters, doesn't she? I've been in that room enough, sweeping and dusting and making up her fire. I've seen her. She puts all the letters in the drawers of the desk, and they aren't locked."

"Oh!" Lottie scrambled up eagerly. "You mean we could go and look? There might be letters there from my father, explaining what happened?"

"I don't think she throws them away." Sally shrugged. "Maybe she burns them, but I've never taken letters out in the waste paper. I don't know how she sorts them, though. Might take us a while to find where they are."

"Let's go now." Lottie snatched up her dressing gown, and Sally huddled her shawl around her shoulders.

"Ssshhh," she murmured, grabbing Lottie's wrist. "You can't go running down the stairs all excited. Calm down, or someone'll hear us. Them stairs creak."

Lottie nodded, leaning against her door frame and taking a few deep, slow breaths. Sally was right. What she wanted to do was fly down the stairs, wrench open Miss Minchin's sitting room door and fling the contents of her desk everywhere. Unless she could compose herself, they would be in more trouble than ever. But – her mother! That she might find out something about her mother, after so long! It was almost impossible to be calm and serious and sensible.

Sally led the way downstairs, carrying her candle and stepping carefully close to the wall, where the steps were less likely to creak. The entrance hall looked huge in the darkness, furniture looming up oddly as Sally passed by with her candle. They slipped inside Miss Minchin's sitting room, tiptoeing past the stiff-backed chairs and making for the desk. It was huge, a wide expanse of dark wood, with lines of drawers all down the sides. Sally held the candle next to it, the light flickering on the brass handles, and despite her excitement even Lottie was somewhat daunted. "How are we ever going to find anything in there?" she murmured, pulling open one of the drawers.

"There must be hundreds and hundreds of letters, look."

"They're parcelled up, though," Sally pointed out, holding the candle closer. "Tied with coloured tape. A bundle for each of you? And labelled, see? We just need to find your label. Mary Abbott, Frances Allan." She picked up a fat package. "Sara Crewe – so she keeps the letters for old pupils too."

Lottie picked through the piles. "No, none of these. Try a few drawers down, if it's alphabetical. Yes, here!" She pounced on a bundle of letters tied with a pink cotton tape.

"Careful." Sally put a hand over hers. "If you don't want her to know we've been here, we need to tie them back up the same way. Look at it first."

Lottie nodded, and then scrabbled at the knotted tape with her nails. It was old and ragged, and she realized that it must have been tied and untied many times before. "They're from my father," she murmured, unfolding the topmost letter and swallowing hard as she held it to the light. It was the one he had sent the day before, angrily reprimanding Miss Minchin for allowing Lottie to fall into bad company. His writing was scratchy and there were several blots, where he had stabbed the pen too hard into the paper.

"Wait a minute." Sally leaned over the drawer again. "There are more in here with your name on."

"Older ones, maybe?" Lottie suggested.

"Mmm. Perhaps. But it looks like different handwriting." Sally handed the parcel to Lottie and held the candle for her to see.

"Yes." It definitely was not the same hand – the writing was curved rather than sharply spiky. Lottie slid off the tape and opened up the first of the letters. The paper was different too, not her father's headed letter paper, but something thinner and more flimsy.

My dearest little girl,

I realize now that you will probably never read this letter.

Your father has told me that there is no point in writing to you at home any longer, as he has sent you to school. He refused to tell me the name of the place, but he told your grandmother – who is equally furious with me, but let out that you are at Miss Minchin's without recognizing what she had done. Of course, you cannot read this yet yourself – I cannot bear to think that I will never see you learning to read, or help you write your first alphabet.

I doubt that anyone will be kind enough to read my letters to you – perhaps they have instructions from your papa not to let you have them at all. Still, even knowing that you may never hear my words, I have to write.

Oh, Lottie, I am sorry that this letter is so confused, my thoughts are in a complete tangle and they have been for weeks, ever since we were torn apart.

I am praying that your father will give in and

let me see you, but he insists that I am a bad influence. He was even cruel enough to say that he will tell you I have died, but I cannot believe that he would do this.

If I had known what would happen – what would I have done? Could I have carried on pretending that all I wanted out of life was to be your father's wife and your mother? I love you so dearly, Lottie, but I cannot sit by quietly and act a role. Perhaps when you are older, you will feel the same way. I hope that you do. Then you will understand why your cruel mamma has abandoned you.

Maybe it is better for you to believe that I am dead, after all. Maybe you will grow up thinking that I did not love you enough to stay. Please believe me, darling Lottie, when I say that I cannot imagine ever loving anyone more. I am not myself, crushed and stifled in your father's house. I cannot love you, or myself, with the weight of all his expectations pressing down on me.

Oh, please understand.

I will write again, my little one.

With all my love,

Mamma

Lottie handed the letter to Sally, her hands shaking. "Read it."

"Lottie, there are . . . maybe a hundred letters here?" Sally murmured, as she read rapidly down the page. "She must have written to you again and again. And Miss Minchin has never given them to you."

"She's not dead."

Sally shook her head. "No." She flicked through the letters to the back of the pile. "Look – this is the last one. Written a few weeks ago. It's only short." She handed it to Lottie.

My Lottie,

This letter is different to all the others. You will see from the horrid thin paper and watery ink that I am not at home or at the office in Lincoln's Inn. Please do not be frightened, darling, when I tell you that I am in prison. I shall not be here for very much longer. I expect that you will not understand and will perhaps be ashamed to have a gaolbird for a mother, but I am very proud to be here.

"She was in prison – it was her, in the newspaper! Sally, I was right. I knew her!"

"What did she do?" Sally asked, her mouth hanging a little open.

Lottie held the letter out to her. "She was trying to present a petition to the prime minister. She was arrested in Downing Street." She brushed her hand across her face, wiping away tears. "Do you think she was on hunger strike? What if they force fed her?"

Sally put the candle down on the desk, her hands shaking, and flung her arms around Lottie. "I don't know. We can't know."

"I'm going to find her," Lottie whispered into her shoulder. "I have to tell her that I could never be ashamed. Never."

"Lottie! Lottie! Oh, thank goodness, there you are." Miss Amelia seized Lottie by the shoulders and twirled her round, inspecting her dress and patting her curls into place. "Your father is here. Yes, you'll do. It isn't the nicest of your dresses, but never mind."

"What?" Lottie blinked, almost sure that she'd misheard.

"You're to go down to Miss Minchin's sitting room."

"My father's *here*?"

"*Yes*, Lottie. Do hurry. He's waiting for you with my sister, in the sitting room."

"But . . . I didn't know that he was coming." Lottie stood, lost, in the middle of her room. She wasn't actually sure she could walk downstairs. She felt as though the floorboards were shaking underneath her.

"Neither did my sister," Miss Amelia said, raising her eyebrows. "She was quite surprised. Do hurry, Lottie, please. They're waiting for you."

She gave Lottie a gentle push and Lottie stumbled out of her room and crept down the stairs, gripping on to the banister tightly.

There were faces peering round the door of the schoolroom, faces that ducked away hurriedly when they saw her looking. The whole school was still full of gossip about what had happened, Lottie realized, but she didn't really care all that much. Miss Amelia opened the door of the sitting room and shooed her in.

Miss Minchin and Lottie's father were sitting in the stiff-backed mahogany armchairs, looking at her as she came through the door.

He looks like the photograph, Lottie thought at first. *Pale and grey and stiff.* And then, *Am I supposed to kiss him?* He felt like a stranger. *I don't love him at all*, she realized, and her stomach seemed to drop inside her. *Perhaps there* is *something awful wrong with me.*

"Good god." He looked her up and down, as if he had expected to see the little nine year old she had been on his last visit. "You're taller."

"I am twelve," Lottie murmured, wondering if he expected her to apologize.

"Yes . . . I suppose you must be," he agreed reluctantly. "You are growing up."

"Do I look like my mother?" Lottie heard herself saying. She didn't even know where the words had come from – they were just there, spilling out of her mouth.

Her father's lips thinned, and he nodded. "Yes. You do."

"How?" Lottie whispered, stepping a little closer to him. "She had hair like mine, didn't she? And blue eyes?"

"Yes. You are very like her."

"I keep dreaming about her, wearing a white dress, and . . . and carrying lilies. I can smell the lilies even when I'm awake sometimes."

He was staring at her, as though she was mad.

"I suppose . . . it must be difficult for you, growing up without knowing her." He forced out the words. "You are greatly to be pitied. But being so unfortunate as to lose your mother does not excuse your behaviour."

He isn't saying it, Lottie thought. *He hasn't actually said that she died. Perhaps he can't say it to me. Perhaps he is ashamed to lie.*

"There are many girls whose mothers have died, who do not take to this kind of" – he shook his head disgustedly – "to these antics."

No. There it was – his hard grey eyes met hers with no sign of shame at all. *I wonder if he told lies to my mother too,* Lottie thought wearily. *He must have had practice – it doesn't seem to be difficult for him at all.*

"Well. I have come to take you out to tea."

Lottie simply gaped at him. It was the last thing she had expected. He had taken her out once before when she was very small, and she had upset a cup of tea into her lap and cried. Her father had hurried her into a cab and back to Miss Minchin's, horrified and embarrassed. She wondered if he remembered. Perhaps he wished that she were little again, so that he need only worry about spilled tea and tears.

"We will be able to have a proper talk. Why don't you go and get yourself ready?" He smiled at her, but his lips looked thin, and Lottie couldn't see any affection in his face. She was sure that there was none in hers.

"Go and fetch your hat, Lottie," Miss Minchin said frostily, and Lottie nodded, confused. The last thing she had been told was that she was not to be allowed out of the seminary, and now she was to go out for a treat? She backed towards the door, eyeing her father like some strange beast, and then turned to drag herself up the stairs.

She was standing in front of the little mirror on her wall, trying to straighten her hat – she couldn't face Miss Minchin telling her off in front of *him* – when there was a sudden knock on the door and Sally flung it open.

"What is it?" Lottie stammered, wondering if her father had changed his mind, and simply gone. She didn't want to spend an hour or so staring at the tablecloth in some smart hotel, listening to him lie.

"Come to say goodbye," Sally muttered, gazing down at the floor.

"What do you mean? He's only taking me out to tea. I'll be back this evening."

Sally looked up, her eyes widening. "Is that what he told you, then?"

"Yes . . . what's happening? What do you know that I don't?"

Sally pushed the door shut behind her, and leaned against it. "Just overheard him telling Miss Minchin not to worry, she'd still get her year's fees, even though he's taking you away now."

"Where?" Lottie whispered, panicked.

"I don't know! Back to your house, I suppose."

"He can't. . ."

"'Course he can. He's your father. It's your home."

"But why would he say that he's taking me out

to tea?" Lottie shook her head. "You must have heard it wrong."

"He said it because he didn't want to drag you out of here kicking and screaming, I reckon." Sally shrugged. "Maybe Miss Minchin told him to. She wouldn't want a scene, would she?"

"I don't want to go with him." Lottie's voice shook. "I don't even know him. He told me my mother was dead, all over again. He said it to my face, looking into my eyes, and I knew he was lying." She took the hat off and laid it on her desk. "I won't go."

"You have to," Sally said doubtfully. "Miss Minchin won't keep you here without his say-so, will she?"

"I know that. I'm not staying here either. I'm going to find my mother. There must be some way I can – that last letter said she had written from the offices in Lincoln's Inn – that's the new WSPU office. Even if I read it wrong, if she's a Suffragette and she's been in prison, they'll know of her at the office, won't they? I'll go there. Someone will tell me how to find her."

Sally shook her head. "What if they don't? Where will you go?"

Lottie bit her bottom lip. "To Sara. I'll go there now and explain. I need my purse. And . . . and perhaps a coat." She looked around the room wildly, trying to think what to take. A clean dress? Her washing things? She couldn't sneak out of the hallway carrying a bag, someone would notice her.

"Your father's in Miss Minchin's sitting room with the door open," Sally said. "You can't just walk out of the door and along the road. Even if you get past him, someone'll see where you've gone. They'll just march round there and snatch you back again."

Lottie clenched her fists and tried to think. She could imagine her father downstairs, pacing Miss Minchin's sitting room. Soon he would send someone after her, she was sure. Perhaps they were already coming up the stairs. . .

"The window! Your window. I'll go across the roof!"

"What?" Sally yelped.

"Ram Dass did it, when the monkey escaped, and then afterwards when he came to bring the furniture and the meals for Sara and Becky. He did it every night, Sara told me. It was her mystery, like a fairy tale. Someone was looking after her when she was so hungry and miserable, and she never knew who it was. All the time it was Ram Dass, climbing out of the attic window at Mr Carrisford's and then in through the window in your bedroom."

"Cook said something about that." Sally peered up at the ceiling. "You reckon you can get across that roof?"

"Yes. It's not far. I've seen it, Sara showed me once, years ago. We fed the sparrows hopping about on the tiles."

"You'd better go then. I'll pack up your things later for you, if you like. Bring them round next door. I can go in and out of the kitchens where you can't."

Lottie nodded, and then suddenly flung her arms around Sally. "I'm not saying goodbye," she whispered croakily. "If I find her, I'll write to you – or I'll write to Ermie and get her to give you the letter. Whatever happens, I'll write, I promise."

Sally nodded, and Lottie saw her eyes brighten with tears. "Don't you forget," the older girl muttered huskily. "I'll never forgive you. We better hurry." She grabbed Lottie's hand and pulled her out into the passageway, glancing along towards the stairs. "No one's coming."

They fled up the attic staircase, barging into Sally's little room. It had been repainted since Sara had lived there – Miss Amelia had insisted. She hardly ever dared to argue with her sister, but after the way they had treated Sara had come out, she had broken down in hysterics. Lottie still remembered her, white and sobbing, drumming her hands on the arms of one of those mahogany chairs. The attic was neatly whitewashed now and the rickety old bed had been replaced. But there was still a wobbly-legged table that could be pulled underneath the skylight. Sally yanked it across the floorboards with a screech and steadied Lottie as she scrambled up.

"Can you open the window?" she asked. "I never have. It might be stuck."

"No. It's coming." Lottie shoved the window up and out, and grabbed the edge, hauling herself up to sit on the window frame, her feet dangling inside.

"What about the house next door? Is there a window open that you can get in?" Sally clambered up on to the table and knelt on it to look.

"It's open a bit. I think I'll be able to pull it." Lottie leaned down and put her arms around Sally's neck. "I *will* see you soon."

"Just be careful," Sally muttered, peering at the slope of the roof. "It makes me feel sick."

"Me too. But I won't go with him. I can't. This

is the only way." Lottie looked at the tiles and caught her breath. "I'm taking my boots off," she murmured, picking at the laces.

"Here, I'll do the other one. Tie them together and put them round your neck. And put your stockings inside them. Bare feet'll grip better."

"It isn't that far," Lottie said, as much to herself as Sally. "Only a few feet. And it isn't really so very steep." She drew her feet up, and gripped the side of the window, climbing out backwards and crouching on the tiles. Then she moved her hand slowly across. In a moment she would have to let go of the window frame. Her boots swung, and knocked against each other, and Lottie heard herself make a little noise, like a whimper.

"Come back in!" Sally hissed. "This is stupid, I'll sneak you through the kitchens somehow."

"No." Lottie let go and lay flat against the tiles. She was filthy with dust and moss already, it didn't matter. She began to wriggle across the roof towards the next-door skylight, while Sally watched. Lottie could hear her breathing, the air catching in her throat. Every time Sally gasped, Lottie felt her heart jump. She fixed her eyes on the tiles in front of her nose, so she couldn't look down at the roof sloping away behind her.

"You're nearly there," Sally called quietly. "You could touch the window, if you reach out."

Keeping her eyes on the rough purple-grey pattern of the tile in front of her, Lottie stretched out her hand, patting it about to find the window frame. Her fingers slipped on smooth painted wood, and she grabbed at it thankfully, and dared to look sideways. Gripping tightly on to the side of the window, she looked down into the room. A servant's bedroom, just as it was on her side, but this one was neatly furnished, with a comfortable bed, and rugs on the painted boards. There was no table under the window; she would have to drop through.

"Are you safe?" Sally called. "Can you get in?"

"Yes!" Lottie yanked at the window, pushing it

further open so she could wriggle in. "Thank you! Goodbye!" She squeezed inside, and there was a thump, and Sally was left staring out across the empty roof, alone.

Chapter Eight

Lottie sat down on the edge of the bed to put her stockings and boots back on. She felt guilty, trespassing in someone else's room, even though she told herself she hadn't a choice. She tiptoed across to the door and twisted the handle slowly so she could peer out. There was a little landing outside, just as there was at Miss Minchin's, and a narrow staircase, with a worn carpet. Lottie crept down, wondering every moment if one of the servants would appear and discover her.

She pressed herself against the wall, hearing

scampering footsteps along the passage below, hoping that whoever it was wouldn't come upstairs. But the little steps came closer and closer, and she tried desperately to think of a way to explain. And then a little ugly furry face popped around the newel post. Lottie laughed.

"You frightened me!" she whispered to the monkey. "I thought you were one of the servants, come to get me into trouble. Where's Sara, Monkey?"

The monkey chattered at her indignantly, obviously surprised to find her there, and Lottie padded quietly down the stairs, whispering gently to him as she had seen Sara do. Eventually he seemed to accept that she was a friend and allowed her to stroke his long brown paw.

"Where's Sara?" Lottie asked him again. "Oh, please, Monkey, I know you're clever. You *can* show me where she is."

The monkey gazed back at her with sad dark eyes, and then turned, loping along the passageway. Lottie stared after him, wondering if he had understood, and he stopped and looked back and gave a little scream, sounding definitely cross.

"Oh! Yes, I'm coming." Lottie hurried after him. They were making for the little sitting room that led off Sara's bedroom, she realized at last, but coming to it from upstairs she hadn't worked out where she was. The monkey swung on the door handle, chattering loudly, and Lottie heard a laugh from inside.

She hurried forward as Sara opened the door.

"Lottie! Whatever are you doing here? What's the matter – what happened to your *dress*?" She caught Lottie's hand and drew her inside to sit down.

"I climbed out of the window – your old window – and across the roof." Lottie slumped into the pretty flowered armchair, her limbs suddenly shaking as what she'd done sank in.

"My father is here," she told Sara. "He's come to

take me away from Miss Minchin's. I couldn't bear it, so I escaped."

"But . . . but . . . you wanted him to come." Sara kneeled beside Lottie's chair, rubbing her cold, scratched hands. "You always said so. You hated that he never saw you." Sara sighed. "I used to envy you, that you had a father at all."

"He lied to me – for years. My mother's still alive. She's been alive all this time and writing to me. I found her letters in Miss Minchin's desk, heartbroken letters. She kept writing even though she knew I'd never answer, that I probably never even saw the letters. I won't go back to him."

"Oh," Sara whispered. She was silent for a moment. Then she said slowly, "Lottie, I don't know if Uncle Tom will hide you. He'll say you should go home to your father."

"I'm not asking him to. Or you. Not for long, anyway. Just . . . just don't tell Miss Minchin that I'm here, when they come to ask. Please. I didn't come in the front of the house, no one knows I'm here but you. And the monkey. All you have to do is let your parlour maid or Ram Dass say that I'm not here." She looked up at Sara pleadingly.

Sara smiled at her, very slightly. "I won't do anything." She held up her hand as Lottie began to plead again. "Lottie, they *know* that you aren't here. They won't ask me, will they? So I shall stay here in my sitting room and know nothing at all." She frowned. "I wonder if I have one of my old dresses, somewhere. That one is only fit for the ragbag now."

"You should tell Mr Carrisford to keep his roof cleaner." Lottie giggled wearily. "I don't think even your outgrown dresses would fit me, but it doesn't matter. Sally is packing me a bag. She said she'll sneak round to the kitchens later. I'm sure Miss Minchin will be here asking questions first, don't worry. No one will have to lie."

"Sally? The maid that you were with when I found you chalking the pavement?" Sara looked worried. "Lottie, it was hardly fair to bring her into this, she will get into the most dreadful trouble."

"She brought me!" Lottie protested. "She was the one who knew all about Suffragettes. I only did it to make Papa angry – at first. And this afternoon it was Sally who came and warned me about him." She laughed sadly. "He'd told me he was taking me out to tea. I expect that actually the cab would have gone straight to the station. Sally heard him talking to Miss Minchin."

"What will you do? I wish you could stay here, but once Uncle Tom finds out what has happened, I know he'll say we must tell your father where you are."

Lottie reached into the pocket of her dress and pulled out the torn sheet of newspaper – the one thing she had brought with her. "This is my mother," she explained simply, handing it to Sara, and pointing at the furthest figure.

Sara read the caption underneath. She looked from the photograph to Lottie and back again, and nodded slowly. "She does look like you. Are you going to try to find her?"

"I'm sure they must know her at the WSPU offices," Lottie said eagerly. "One of her letters said something about writing from there. I think she must work for the WSPU. Maybe it was my mother wanting rights for women that made her and father separate. I didn't have a chance to read all of her letters and I couldn't take them with me in case Miss Minchin saw they were gone, but she talked about not being able to be herself and not wanting to be only a wife and mother." She saw that Sara was looking doubtful. "You must see! What if someone said that you couldn't possibly become a writer, because you're a girl?"

Sara laughed. "Uncle Tom would defend me to the last – but he still doesn't think I should be able to vote. He thinks it should be enough that he votes for me. I don't know, Lottie. I . . . I respect your mother, fighting for her principles, being brave enough to be sent to prison. I think women are clever enough to understand about the world, of course I do. And if we're to work like men, why shouldn't we vote like them? But smashing windows, and setting buildings on fire . . . I can't understand how that can be right."

"That's what Sally said. But my mother – Mamma – she was trying to give a petition to the prime minister. She didn't hurt anyone." Lottie sat up straighter. "And even if she had, I would still want to see her and talk to her. You can understand that, can't you?"

Sara squeezed her hands tighter. "Of course. I'll help you find her, I promise."

A faint clanging sound echoed below and Lottie flinched. The front door bell – it was almost certain to be Miss Minchin, come searching for her. She turned wide, panicked eyes on Sara, who patted her hands comfortingly, and then crept to the door. She opened it, the door swinging back without a creak on well-oiled hinges, and beckoned to Lottie, and the two girls leaned around it to listen.

"No, ma'am." Lottie could hear the surprise in the parlour maid's voice. "No, Miss Sara hasn't had any visitors at all today." A pause, and Miss Minchin's voice, too far away to hear the words from out on the front step, but obviously irritated. "Well, I don't know, I'm sure, ma'am. She hasn't been here. Yes, ma'am. If we see her. Good day." The parlour maid shut the door with a crisp bang, and Sara and Lottie could hear her muttering to herself. Miss Minchin had clearly not troubled to be particularly polite.

Sara closed the door carefully, and they breathed a sigh of relief. "I wonder if she believed Lucy?" Sara murmured. "We'll have to be careful. Sit down, Lottie. I'll order some tea – I can drink out of my tooth mug, I don't mind. Oh!"

Lottie jumped out of the armchair as a soft knock sounded at the door, and Sara pressed her finger to her lips, and waved her towards the other door, which led to her bedroom. Lottie darted inside and waited, her heart racing. What if Miss

Minchin hadn't trusted Lucy? Perhaps it was her father on the other side of the door?

"Come in!"

Ram Dass opened the door and bowed solemnly to Sara. "Missee Sahib," he murmured. "Young lady is here to see you." Then he stepped back, and ushered Sally into the room, white-faced and miserable-looking, and carrying a brown-paper parcel.

"Thank you, Ram Dass." Sara waited until he had closed the door, and then came forward, smiling at Sally. "Did you come round the back of the house? Oh, and those must be Lottie's things. She's very lucky to have you helping her, she can't keep on wearing that pink dress, it's completely ruined."

Lottie burst out from behind the bedroom door. "What's the matter? Have you been crying?"

Sally shook her head. "No. Only a little bit anyway." She hugged the parcel to her grubby coat. "This isn't yours, it's mine. Miss Minchin found me packing up your dress and washing things and she worked out that I'd warned you. She sacked me. No references. I've got my wages, but I'll have to spend it on a train fare back to Barkingside. If they'll take me. And I couldn't bring anything of yours out of the house with me."

"That doesn't matter." Lottie shook her head. "Oh, Sally . . . I thought you'd be safe. Sara was right – she said I should never have dragged you into this. I'm sorry."

Sally shrugged. "Didn't have to help you, did I? It was me that got caught."

"Did anyone see you coming in?" Sara asked, pushing the chair from her little writing table over by the armchairs. "Sit down."

"Thank you, miss. And no, I'd swear to it. I waited on the other side of the square till it was all clear."

"I will be able to find you a new place, I'm sure." Sara told her. "You can stay here till we do. I promise I'll find something."

"Or we could talk to Miss Bailey from the WSPU shop," Lottie suggested suddenly. "She might be able to find somewhere they didn't mind you being a Suffragette. So you wouldn't have to keep sneaking around."

"What about you, then?" Sally asked. "I saw Miss Minchin marching along the road to look for you – I ducked down the area steps on one of the houses on the other side so she wouldn't see me."

"Lucy told her I hadn't been here. Did you see my father, Sally? Is he still at Miss Minchin's?"

"No. He stalked out looking like a thundercloud, about half an hour after Miss Minchin came here." Sally sniggered. "She must have had to tell him that she hadn't a clue where you were."

Sara frowned. "He's probably worried. I wonder if he will call in the police."

"I should think he's just furious." Lottie found that she had wrapped her arms around her middle and made herself put them down, folding her hands neatly in her lap, a picture of ladylike behaviour. "He will definitely be furious. But I don't care." She looked down at her torn, stained dress, and sighed. "Sara, can I borrow something to wear after all? I think we should go to Lincoln's Inn now. As soon as possible." She squeezed her hands tight. Her father couldn't suspect that she had found out his lies, surely? But there was nowhere else to look for her. "I have to find my mamma before he does," she said suddenly. "Before he bursts in on her, demanding to know where I am." She looked pleadingly between Sally and Sara. "Will you come with me? Please?"

"'Course I will." Sally nodded, and Sara sprang up.

"I'm going to order the car. Uncle Tom bought the same model that we took to . . . to the races." Her voice dropped a little. "Then I'll come back and find you a dress. You two can nip out of the door into the alley at the back of the house, and when I see you walking along, I shall tell the chauffeur to pick you up. We are going shopping in the Strand, that's perfectly respectable."

Lottie stood by the desk, holding out the photograph, trying not to let the clerk in front of her see that she was about to cry. She felt childish and silly enough as it was, in Sara's too-long, too-tight dress.

"Would it be possible to show someone else?" Sara asked politely. "Some of the other ladies?"

"I'm sorry, I can't allow you to go traipsing round the office." The clerk shook her head. "We're very busy."

"Please!" Lottie gasped, brushing her hand across her eyes, but the telephone was ringing and the clerk began to speak into it hurriedly. She didn't even bother to wave them away.

"We'll come back tomorrow," Sara whispered, putting an arm around Lottie's waist and smiling at Sally as she found her doing the same thing. They drew Lottie out into the entrance hall together.

"What if I never find her?" Lottie hiccupped. "I haven't anywhere to go! I can't stay with you, you can't hide me upstairs, it's stupid. I can't bear to go back to Miss Minchin and my father now. He'll never let me out again! I'll never see either of you. Miss Minchin will have told him that you're a terrible influence, Sara, even if he doesn't work out where I was."

"It'll be different tomorrow," Sara suggested soothingly, as they came out on to Kingsway and she looked up and down the road for the car. "They were busy. We *will* find someone who knows her, Lottie. And if necessary I shall hire a private detective," she added suddenly. Then she smiled at Lottie's shocked face. "Why not? I'm sure we can find one, the newspapers are full of advertisements."

"It'll come right," Sally whispered, but Lottie gasped and tore herself out of their hold.

"What is it?" Sara cried, and she tried to catch Lottie's hand, but Lottie was already racing away down the road.

"Her father," Sally said grimly, nodding towards a cab that had pulled up just short of the WSPU offices. "She was right, he did come after her. We'd better follow her."

"Lottie, come here," her father called, marching down the street towards Sally and Sara. His face was scarlet, and clearly he was hideously embarrassed to be shouting after his daughter in one of the busiest streets in London.

Lottie looked back at him, and then darted out across the road, between two horse-drawn delivery carts.

"Lottie, no!" Sally shrieked, dashing forward, but it was too late. The car swerved, the driver yelling out in horror, and Lottie tried to dodge, but she couldn't get away. Sally and Sara clutched at each other and watched as the front wing caught Lottie a glancing blow, flinging her into the road.

"Lottie! My god." Lottie's father strode into the middle of the street, where the driver of the car was climbing out. "What were you thinking? That's my daughter!"

"She . . . she ran in front of me. . ." the man stammered. "I couldn't stop in time. I'm so sorry – but she was . . . she was just there. . ."

"Better get her out of the road, sir," one of the cart drivers suggested, as Sara and Sally threaded their way through the cars and drays. "Cause another accident, all piled up here like this. You watch out, missy," he added, fending off one of his horses from Sara.

"Yes. . ." Lottie's father bent down, scooping her up. Sally pressed her hand against her mouth as she saw Lottie limp and sagging in his arms.

"Her head is bleeding," Sara murmured anxiously, as they followed him to the edge of the road. "Is she breathing?"

Lottie's father glared at her as he laid Lottie on the pavement, and a small knot of people began to gather. "You are the girl Miss Minchin told me of! You encouraged her in all this – and I suppose you had your servants lying for you!"

Sara drew herself up straighter, and stared at him, her grey-green eyes sharp as stones. "Yes, I lied. One lie. How many have you told to Lottie, over the years? Do you know why she ran away from you? She'd discovered the truth, that her mother had been alive all this time, and you had separated them. And now you have chased after her and terrified her so much that she may never see her mother after all!" She ran her hand over Lottie's face and pulled off the silk motoring scarf she was wearing, using it to blot the bleeding cut on her cheek.

"What rubbish. . ." Mr Legh said feebly, glancing back at the men standing over him and Lottie. "I'm sure she will be perfectly all right. She's breathing, look. And she has always had the very best of care. Lottie is just a spoiled little girl – and she has been under a bad influence."

Sally looked up from where she was kneeling

next to Lottie's head and snorted. "You can't have it both ways."

"I beg your pardon?" Mr Legh asked, his voice full of outraged stiffness. "And who, exactly, are you?"

But Sally half stood up, staring past him, her mouth dropping open. "Miss Sara, look!" She pointed down the street, and Sara turned.

"Is that her?" She looked at the photograph, torn and dirtied now, but still clutched in Lottie's hand.

"That photograph," Lottie's father snarled. "Is that how she knew?"

"She'd dreamed of her mother for years," Sally told him. "She knew that there was something not right. Lottie would have found her mother somehow, however many times you lied to her."

"I will not let that woman near my daughter!" Mr Legh's face had grown so red, that one of the carters put a hand on his arm, clearly worried that he was about to collapse in a fit of rage.

"Too late," Sally muttered, her lips curving in a smile of grim triumph.

Mr Legh wheeled around and hissed, like a tea kettle. "You!"

The woman approaching Lincoln's Inn House saw him and recoiled, her face going white. "Harry . . . you followed me here? What on earth do you want now? Is this another vile ploy from your lawyers?" Then her eyes travelled over the little group – the driver of the car, the two draymen, Sara and Sally, the whispering passers-by – and then the pathetic little heap of dusty blue cloth between them all. "Good gracious, what happened? Harry, did you knock a child down? Have you sent someone for a doctor? Is she very badly hurt?" Her face seemed to grow even whiter as she hurried closer, crouching down beside Lottie. She stretched out one hand, not quite daring to touch Lottie's bright hair.

"It's her," Sally said. "I'm so sorry, ma'am. We came to look for you, she was sure she'd find you here, but we couldn't get properly inside to ask."

"There have been so many people trying to attack the offices . . . we have to be so cautious. . ." Lottie's mother murmured, but it was obvious that she was speaking almost at random. She had eyes only for Lottie. She slipped one hand under Lottie's shoulders, lifting her so that Lottie lay in her lap. "Oh, my darling. . ." She looked up at Sara and Sally. "You came with her to find me?"

"She was running away, ma'am," Sally explained, looking sideways at Lottie's father. "He was going to take her out of the school and back home with him. She'd not seen him for a good many years and she was desperate. She told me she belonged to no one. You see, she did truly believe that you had died, but still she dreamed of you. She told me the dreams."

"What was she doing, talking about our family affairs to a servant?" Mr Legh demanded, puffing up red again. "I will have that Minchin woman prosecuted. It seems my daughter has been abandoned to find her companions below stairs."

"Is that all you can say?" Sara's voice was full of disgust. "If you cared for Lottie at all, you would be running to fetch a doctor to her!"

"Poor little love," one of the draymen muttered. "Torn away from her ma."

"Seems like someone should be fetching the police and all," the other driver agreed.

"What?" Lottie's father shouted. "This is ridiculous! Good god, can we not take her inside, away from all these gawking idiots?"

"Of course," Lottie's mother said swiftly, and she looked hopefully up at the two carters. "Would you mind helping me? I don't think I can lift her easily and I don't want to risk jarring her poor head." She pressed Sara's scarf close against Lottie's face, and the man who had called Lottie a poor little love scooped her up, tiny in his arms. "In here, then?" he asked, making for the grand door of the WSPU.

"No!" Lottie's father exclaimed. "Of course not!" But the man was already walking away, Lottie's mother at his side, and Sara and Sally pressing close, and Mr Legh was forced to hurry after them.

"Anne, would you telephone for a doctor?" Lottie's mother called, as she directed the carter to lay Lottie down on a padded bench in the entrance hall.

"Miss Walker?" The clerk who had ignored Lottie beforehand jumped up, staring at them in shock. "Oh, no . . . these girls – they were looking for *you*. I didn't realize. . ."

"A doctor, please," Lottie's mother waved away the clerk's horrified apologies. "I think she may be coming around, don't you?" She glanced from Sara to Sally, both kneeling on the marble floor next to the bench. "Her eyelids are twitching, I'm sure – there, look!"

"Yes!" Sally grabbed Lottie's dusty hand. "Oh, thank god, miss. Lottie!"

Lottie blinked again, and looked up at Sally and Sara, their anxious faces leaning over her. "My father..." she whispered fearfully. "He's here, I saw him. We have to get away."

"How can you talk like this?" Mr Legh growled. "You're just like her. After I did everything I could to school her influence out of you! I was assured that everything would be done to bring you up as a model child, and instead I have another little criminal."

"Perhaps it would have worked better if you had tried to do it yourself, instead of paying someone else to do it for you..." Lottie's mother moved so that Lottie could see her. "Lottie, darling. You won't know—"

"Mamma?" Lottie whispered, unbelievingly. She looked between Sara and Sally, confused, and not daring to hope.

"It really is her," Sara promised. "You were right."

Lottie reached out, holding up the ragged piece of newspaper, and her mother took it.

"Oh, Lottie. This is all you had? Harry, you never even let her have a photograph?"

"You're dead to me," Lottie's father said coldly. "I

heard that woman call you Miss Walker. You don't even carry my name. You were dead to Lottie, as you should be."

"You can't – not now that I know," Lottie whispered shakily. "I'll find her, whatever you do. I'll run away, again and again."

Her father stared down at her in disgust. "Perhaps I should have let her keep you, as she wanted."

"Did you want to?" Lottie breathed, moving her head painfully to look at her mother.

"Oh, Lottie, of course I did! I begged and begged, but I had so little money, and my family were as angry with me as he was. They wouldn't help me pay for a lawyer. My father and brothers told me that any court would always give you to him, and I wasn't brave enough to fight for you as I should have done. They told me that if I did as I was told, he would let me see you, that you would have my letters – but then he locked you away from me entirely. I have never regretted anything more. I should have fought, I should have done everything I could to keep you."

"He lied," Lottie whispered. "To you as well."

"I will not stay here and listen to this," Lottie's father said bitterly. "So you want to stay with your disgrace of a mother? Good luck to the pair of you."

"Harry – you'll let me keep her?" Lottie's mother stood up slowly. "You mean it?"

He glared at her, and then sighed shakily, rubbing his hand across his face. "You don't understand how angry I was," he muttered. "The way everyone was talking. The whispers... I couldn't let you win!"

"She's not a—" Lottie's mother started to say, but then she pressed her lips together, as if to stop herself. "Thank you. I will write to you, of course, with news of Lottie. She will write herself, I'm sure."

"I'll speak to the lawyers." Lottie's father stared at her. "And that blasted school, I suppose. I have to go." He glanced disgustedly around the marble hall. "Goodbye, Lottie."

"Goodbye." Lottie found that her voice was shaking, even though she couldn't remember ever feeling happier. "I will write, I promise."

And he was gone, leaving only her mother, and Sara and Sally, leaning over her and stroking her forehead, frowning and murmuring about doctors.

"It feels like another dream." Lottie closed her eyes and opened them again.

"I can pinch you, if you want," Sally offered, and Lottie giggled faintly.

"I can't smell lilies, though."

"Lilies?" Lottie's mother glanced worriedly at the two older girls. "What does she mean? Is she delirious? Where is that doctor?"

"When she was very small, and we all thought that you were dead, I told her a story about our mothers, that they were somewhere beautiful, with fields and fields of lilies," Sara explained.

"She always dreamed of you with your arms full of them," Sally agreed. "All their golden dust scattered down your dress."

Lottie's mother sat back, her face full of shock. "The last day," she whispered. "But she was so tiny! She can't even have been three, how could she remember?"

Lottie hauled herself up with an effort. "It was real? You were gathering lilies?"

"Harry and I fought, because I had the pollen all over my hands, and there was a guest, oh, someone he wanted me to impress. It was just the same fight all over again." Lottie's mother pressed her hands against her eyes. "You were with me in the garden. Why didn't I pick you up and take you with me, Lottie? Instead of telling your nanny to take you back to the nursery?" She let out a shaky breath and dropped her hands. "We could have had years."

"Oh. . ." Sally gulped. "I'm sorry, miss. It's too sad."

"Mamma," Lottie's voice wavered as she said it. "This isn't the right time, I know, but you have to help Sally find a new position. In a house with a family that doesn't mind she's a Suffragette. Miss Minchin sacked her this morning because she was trying to help me get away."

"Since you're well enough to think of that, I can't believe you climbed over a roof and didn't do any more than tear your dress, and then you go running into a road and get yourself half-killed! I could slap you," Sally said crossly, sniffing. "Please don't worry about me, miss."

"But I do," Lottie's mother shook her head. "I want to know everything. You climbed over a roof, Lottie? You must tell me exactly what happened – how you found the letters, all of it. Once a doctor has seen Lottie, you must all come home with me."

"Home?" Lottie wriggled until she was sitting upright. "See, I'm not half-killed at all, Sally, just my head aches a little. Do you have a house – or . . . or rooms somewhere? I wouldn't mind what it was. But I can live there with you?"

"I share a house with a friend who works here

too, and you will most certainly live there with me."

Her mother stroked her cheek, and then smiled at Sally. "You too, until we can find what would be best for you for you to do. Another position, if you like, or perhaps something here."

Sally swallowed, looking around the marble hall, and at the women hurrying purposefully past them. She ducked her head, but Lottie could see that her lips were sucked in to stop herself from crying or laughing, or perhaps both. She put her hand in Sally's.

"A home."

Sally nodded. "I can't believe it's real."

"Nor me." Lottie shook her head. "The first time I ever saw you, when you were standing on the area steps, that's what I was thinking about, that I didn't have anyone or anywhere that was really mine. Even though Sara had promised to be my mother."

Sara hugged her. "It's all right. I shall give you back."

Lottie's mother watched Sara and Sally, their arms around her lost daughter, lost and found. "Lottie, I don't think you knew how lucky you were."

Author's Note

On 21st January 2017, while I was writing the second draft of this book, I went on the Women's March in London with my thirteen-year-old son, Tom. Between eighty and a hundred thousand women, men and children marched in protest against attacks on women's rights in the US, in solidarity with two and a half million marchers worldwide.

Then I came back home and went on working on *The Princess and the Suffragette*, feeling that it was more important than ever to talk about women and their struggle to win the vote. The procession that Lottie and Ermengarde watch in Chapter Two was real – it was the Women's Coronation Procession, in 1911. This procession of sixty thousand Suffragette supporters must have been an incredible experience for those taking part. When I wrote that Lottie felt it was beautiful and exciting just to have been there, it echoes the way Tom and I felt over a hundred years later. What's so sad is that we were marching for the same reasons – to say that women and men are equal, and should be treated equally. That women should have the right to say what happens to their own bodies. That women should never feel that they are controlled by their partners, fathers or governments.

There were even women dressed as Suffragettes on the march in 2017 – their costumes and signs clever and desperately sad all at the same time.

However we feel now about the Suffragettes' violent means of protest – and you can probably tell from the conversations between Lottie and

Sally that I find it hard to work out how I feel, even after writing this book – we cannot forget that their fight is still going on, and we are all still a part of it.

Holly Webb, 2017

Read Holly Webb's magical sequel to another of Frances Hodgson Burnett's timeless classics…

Return to the Secret Garden

Holly Webb